Calling Invisible Women

Calling Invisible Women

A Novel

Jeanne Ray

Crown Publishers

New York

Published in the United States by Crown Publishers, an imprint of the Crown Publishing Group, a division of Random House, Inc., New York.
www.crownpublishing.com

CROWN and the Crown colophon are registered trademarks of Random House, Inc.

Library of Congress Cataloging-in-Publication Data
Ray, Jeanne.
Calling invisible women : a novel / Jeanne Ray.—1st ed.
p. cm.
1. Women—Fiction. 2. Domestic fiction. I. Title
PS3568.A915C35 2012
813'.54—dc23
2011037169

ISBN 978-0-307-39505-4
eISBN 978-0-307-95551-7

Printed in the United States of America

Jacket design and illustration by Maria Elias

10 9 8 7 6 5 4 3 2 1

First Edition

To my friend,

Jemima Perry.

She was never invisible,

nor will she be.

still wasn't there. My toothbrush was there, floating by itself several inches out from the cuff of my robe, and the robe was there, the collar and shoulders filling out the bottom of the mirror's frame, but *I* was missing. I moved from side to side a couple of times trying to fit myself back into the picture, but all I saw was the open shower curtain behind me, the tiles of the tub, the built-in shelf that held the shampoo and conditioner. I spat out the toothpaste and there it was in the sink looking exactly like toothpaste. That was when I thought: *stroke*. Pieces of my vision were missing, even though I couldn't imagine what kind of stroke would just remove a face, a neck, a hand. Leaning forward toward the mirror, I gently tapped my invisible fingers against my invisible cheek and what had once been a finger was stopped by what had once been a face. Curiosity was quickly being replaced by a rising wall of panic. I was fifty-four years old, and I was gone.

"Red?" I said, trying out my voice. Unlike the rest of me, my voice was still there. Red lifted his head from the bath mat and looked straight at me, his brown eyes bright and full of recognition. He wagged his tail, thinking that maybe I wanted to go for another walk. Tentatively, I held out my invisible hand to him, wondering if I was dead and, if I was, what effect it would have on the poor dog. But Red sniffed the place where my hand should have been and gave it a couple of licks. I felt the rough wash of his tongue working over my phantom wrist, which I took to be a good sign, and so I went back to the mirror again. Still not there.

I went into the bedroom feeling light-headed, or feeling like someone who didn't have a head, and, sitting down on the edge of the bed (which gave a creak of recognition), I picked up the phone and dialed the back-line number at Arthur's office. I suppose that any day one finds one's self to be invisible was not going to shape up to be a lucky day, so when Arthur's nurse Mary answered I shouldn't have been surprised. Arthur has three nurses and getting Mary on the phone was the definite equivalent of drawing the short straw.

"Dr. Hobart's office," she said, impatient from the start.

"Mary, it's Clover. I need to speak to Arthur." I was struggling not to hyperventilate.

I could see her shaking her head. "He's in with a patient. Is there something I can help you with?"

Maybe she thought I was calling in regard to a sick child, even though she knew that Nick was twenty-three and Evie was twenty. "Can you get him for me?"

"He has patients waiting in all five of the exam rooms with fourteen more in the waiting room." Her voice was both flat and brisk. "He's in with the mayor's wife now. Their second-grader has a rash. It could be a tick bite. We've got a vomiting toddler in room three and a first-time mother in room one who has brought in a week's worth of used diapers that she has been refrigerating because she thinks the stool is inconsistent."

"I get it," I said, though there was nothing even notable about her report. This was Arthur's day, all day, every day, from the minute he walked in the door of his office until the minute he left, and even when he left, much of his work managed to follow him home. I understood it was her job to protect him in any way possible, to use herself to create a human shield between him and the world, but I never did appreciate the fact that she applied that same shield against me. I almost never called the office.

"Is it an emergency?" Mary asked.

"It is."

"Okay," she said, but I could tell she had already been distracted. I could hear a shrill screaming in the background, and then, abruptly, the line went dead.

So there I was, the phone levitating in midair. I stared at it for a minute before hanging up. Even if I'd gotten Arthur on the line he no doubt would have told me that children don't become invisible and so he wouldn't know anything about it. Arthur had a way of making it sound like he had attended some special sort of junior medical school at which he had received absolutely no information whatsoever about the human body past the age of sixteen. It was his means of deflecting grown-ups who casually hit him up for Adderall prescriptions at dinner parties, but it also meant he never was much of a help to the adult members of his own family.

And who's to say I was invisible anyway? If I was cracking up, if I'd just suffered some sort of cerebral hemorrhage, I would in fact be a poor judge of the situation. I tightened the belt on my robe and I marched up the stairs to Nick's room, Red right behind me. I could feel my bare feet against the floor. Nick is our oldest, and I opened the door to his room without knocking because he had gone away to college and stayed away for almost two years after graduating. I had made his room my office: a desk, a lamp, a chair. My mother had made my room a sewing room when I moved away. Now my computer was back in the kitchen. "Nick!" I said to the man who was sleeping face down and shirtless in a pile of crumpled sheets. "Nicky, wake up!"

When he didn't wake up I took hold of his heel with my invisible hand and shook it. I could see his entire leg turning back and forth inside the flannel pajama bottoms I had bought for him two Christmases ago; I could feel the heat of his heel in my palm. Red jumped into the bed and stood for a moment on Nick's back. In our household, only Red had experienced unequivocal joy at Nick's return.

"What?" he said into his pillow. It wasn't quite eight in the morning. It was for Nick an unseen hour.

"I need you to look at me."

"You look fine," he said, or I think that's what he said. He hadn't lifted his head.

I flicked the switch to the overhead lights, and then I went to the windows and snapped up the rolling shades. With admirably quick reflexes, Nick drew himself into a ball and howled the howl of all vampires exposed to sunlight. In the light I could see that the room, which I had told him he would have to clean himself when he moved home six months ago, had not been cleaned. He scrunched his pillow down over the back of his head while Red buried his nose into the covers in search of Nick's nose.

"What?" he cried, either to me or the dog.

"I need you to tell me if you can see me." I was trying to keep my voice steady but I could hear the panic.

He rolled over, blinking in my general direction. The light was burning his eyes. He pressed his chin down to his chest, lengthening his neck like a turtle. "What's this about?"

"Do. You. See. Me."

"You don't like your bathrobe anymore? You want to know if it's becoming? I don't know what you're asking."

"How can you not know what I'm asking? Am I here?"

Nick had been a history major at Oberlin, and though we had begged him to consider a minor in business, he had gone for women's studies instead. Women's studies, he informed us at the time, was a brilliant way to meet girls. "Are you having some sort of breakdown?"

"I might be." My robe was shaking.

"If you feel like I don't appreciate you, well," he said, rubbing his eyes, "it's because I don't. I will again, but not until at least ten, okay?" He put his arm over the dog and pulled him in tight like a wide receiver ready for a forty-yard run. "Please pull the shades on your way out."

That was when I turned and looked in the mirror over his dresser. There I was, my hair dripping and uncombed but recently touched up for gray, my cheeks bright red from a combination of fear and rosacea. I was back, so completely and utterly returned it was as if I had never been gone at all.

.   .   .

Maybe it was just some weird aphasia, except instead of a temporary loss of speech I had experienced a selective loss of vision. As I dried my hair and put on the little bit of makeup that I associated with my own human dignity, I stared hard at my reflection, checking for any fuzziness or missing spots. Even after I was dressed I kept going back to the mirror to make sure I was still there. I couldn't spend more than two minutes away. Sure, I could see my hands, my legs, but was my face still there? My neck? Back I would go to check again. Spending a morning staring at oneself was hardly the short path to peace of mind. It was the mirror, after all, that had driven Snow White's step-mother around the bend with its unrelentingly frank assess-ment of the situation. Soon my worry about invisibility had been replaced by a cataloguing of flaws: my eyelids were drooping in a weird way that made my entire face look asymmetrical, and the crease between my eyebrows made me look as if I had been struck in the forehead by a very small ax. And my mouth! Where had my lips disappeared to over the years? I preferred the picture of myself I kept in my imagination, the one in which my hair could still be braided into a thick rope and I was in the neighborhood of thirty-five.

I went across the street and three houses down to the Kemptons'. I knocked on Gilda's door.

"Have you ever noticed that my eyelids are uneven?" I asked her. I was standing on the porch. There was a cold wind prying the last of the red leaves off the maple tree in her front yard and I shivered. *That time of year thou mayst in me behold when yellow leaves, or none, or few, do hang.*

"Come inside," she said. She put her hands on my shoulders and moved me around in the light as if she was having trouble seeing me.

Upon those boughs which shake against the cold. Bare ruined choirs, where late the sweet birds sang.

"I need to get my glasses," she said.

Gilda and Steve Kempton had five children, all of them boys, and their house always had the vague aura of a summer camp, even though four of those boys were technically grown and three of them were actually gone. There were always helmets and hockey sticks in the front hallway, always an odd number of tennis shoes on the stairs. In the summer the floors had a vaguely sandy crunch to them even though we lived in Ohio, and nowhere near a beach. Benny, the baby, was in high school now, and Miller, who was the second to the oldest, had boomeranged straight back into his childhood bedroom the day after graduating from college and had been there for more than a year. I believed that it was Miller who set the bad example for Nick.

Gilda came back with a pair of readers and, looking through her glasses, gave my eyelids serious consideration. Then she put her thumb between my eyebrows and made little circles over the crease there. "I tried that," I said. "It doesn't go away."

"Botox." She tapped her own forehead, a smooth lake of tranquillity.

"I did that once. You know I don't like needles. And anyway, the wrinkles grew back."

She shrugged and looked again. "You don't really notice it," she said, but not in a way that made me feel better. Gilda and I had been friends for twelve years, ever since we'd moved into the neighborhood. It was her honesty that I counted on. If I needed a comforting lie I was perfectly capable of telling one to myself. She was walking into the kitchen, stepping over a couple of tennis racquets, and I followed her. She put the kettle on.

"So if you aren't interested in needles, why are you making an assessment of your face? Your only two options are to fix it or live with it. There's no point in just beating yourself up about it."

"The thing is," I started tentatively, not knowing how to talk about what I wasn't really sure had happened, "this morning—" I stopped.

Gilda, that source of constant motion, stopped as well. "This morning," she said. I could tell she was thinking I was about to give her bad news.

"I was invisible."

Gilda turned and got down two cups from the cabinet beside the sink, let out a dispirited sigh, and then dropped a tea bag in each of those cups. "I hate that."

Something in my spine caught a small jolt of current and straightened to attention—it was understanding, recognition. It was everything I was hoping for. "It's happened to you?"

Gilda lowered her chin and looked up at me, a move I now realized was meant to stand in for a knitted brow. "Are you kidding me? Except for a very few breakout moments, I've been invisible since the new millennium. The boys can be looking at naked women on Facebook and they don't so much as twitch when I walk into the room. I can ask Steve what time he wants to eat dinner and he keeps on texting like I wasn't even there. A woman wheels her cart right in front of mine and cuts into the checkout lane, a car cuts me off in traffic, I wave at the waiter and he's looking at the wall behind my head. It's just the plight of women after a certain age. No one can see you. Sometimes I find myself daydreaming about that girl I used to be, how I could always get a table in a busy restaurant. I could raise my hand on a street corner in New York in the pouring rain and get a taxi." She shook her head at such an impossible memory. "That's just gone now. We're nothing but the ghosts of our former selves."

"True," I said. I had forgotten the feeling of going into a very busy restaurant at eight on a Friday night and getting a table without a reservation. "But that's not what I'm talking about."

"So what are you talking about?"

"Invisibility. Literal invisibility." I sounded less than certain. Gilda and I told each other pretty much everything but I found these words were heavy in my mouth.

"You mean where you walk right up to someone and it's as if they can't even see you?"

"No, where I look in the mirror and can't see myself."
There was nothing metaphorical about it.

"Does this have to do with Arthur?"

"He wasn't even there. It was after he'd left for work."

"No, but I mean he's been very busy lately. You've said it
yourself. You hardly ever see him."

"Which is not the same thing as hardly ever seeing myself. Do you think this is hysterical invisibility? I'm develop-
ing some strange new disease in an effort to get the doctor's
attention? The only way I could get Arthur's attention, med-
ically speaking, is with a bad case of cradle cap."

"He can't help how busy he is," Gilda said defensively.
"He's busy because he's good. He's busy because everybody
loves him."

Everybody including Gilda. Not long after we'd moved
into the neighborhood, Arthur dislodged a grape from Benny's windpipe at a Fourth of July party and saved his life.
Arthur had noticed that Benny, who was only three at the
time, was standing stock-still in the middle of a crowd of
adults, just standing there, not even blinking. Arthur said
later he knew something was wrong because he'd never
seen Benny stand still before. He grabbed the boy's ankles
and, flipping him over in midair, shook him like a pillow-
case. Out popped the grape, which was followed by the
enormous wail the grape had blocked in his throat. With
a little cajoling, Benny got over the shock of it almost immediately. Gilda never did. "This has nothing to do with
Arthur," I said.

"Okay." Gilda tilted her head slightly to the side. "So can you see yourself now?"

"Of course I can see myself now." I held out my arm to show us both. "I'm not delusional, at least I don't think I am. I got out of the shower this morning and for a few minutes I couldn't see myself."

"I don't think I'd mind that," Gilda said.

I threw up my hands. "I swear to you this isn't coming around to a punch line. I can't explain what happened, but it did happen, and then it was over. I guess I was just wondering . . ."

"Wondering what?"

"If it ever happened to you."

The kettle let out its high-pitched wail and Gilda rescued it from the flame and filled our cups. "No," she said tentatively. "Not if we're talking about a lack of physical matter. Have you had your eyes checked?"

I shook my head.

"I wonder if French women ever feel invisible," she said, deftly trying to steer the subject away from the personal and toward the cultural. "People are always talking about how chic and secure French women are, but if the twenty-year-old Brigitte Bardot passed the seventy-six-year-old Brigitte Bardot on the street, there isn't going to be any contest as to who gets noticed."

That was when I came to the conclusion that feeling invisible was something that could be talked about for hours on end but being invisible was a conversational no-man's-land. I blew on my tea and looked at my watch. "I should probably get to work. I've got a column due. Is it okay if I just take the cup with me?"

"Of course you can take the cup, but I haven't been any help at all." Gilda sounded genuinely sorry.

I waved her off. "I'm fine," I said. "I just needed to talk." In truth, maybe Gilda had been more of a help than she had realized. Maybe I had suffered a brief bout of insanity and by not acknowledging it, she was allowing me to keep my dignity. I had no real idea what had happened. I just had a strange, unsettled feeling, like you do when you're out and think you might have left the oven on or the windows open in the rain. Later, of course, I found out this feeling was all part of it. Some of the women in the group call it an invisibility hangover, like every cell you've got has had a tiny whiplash from coming back into focus again.

When I got back to the house, Nick was sitting at the kitchen table eating a bowl of cereal, and Red, who didn't even turn his face in my direction when I came in, was staring up at him. Nick always let Red lap up the last of the milk when he was finished with it. "You're stirring awfully early," I said without thinking.

"Thank you very much for that," he said. "What was up with you this morning anyway?"

"This morning?" I asked, not wanting to do it all again.

"Do you see me?" Nick said, mimicking my panic in an

unbecoming manner. He was working the crossword puzzle in the *Times*. His father must have been in a rush this morning. Since Nick had come home, Arthur usually remembered to hide the arts section so that he wasn't left with the pathetic puzzle in the local paper.

"My contact lens was stuck," I said, coming up with a slightly plausible lie. "I think I'm going to have to stop wearing them. My optometrist says I have dry eyes."

"You don't wear contact lenses, and even if you did, what would that have to do with whether or not I can see you?" He filled in an answer with a ballpoint pen. It was the Thursday puzzle. Not easy.

"I said, 'I can't see.' I'm sorry. I just panicked for a minute."

"You didn't say, 'I can't see.' You said, 'Can you see me?' There's a difference. Mid-arthropod, six letters."

"Do you have anything?"

"Starts with *T*."

The *T* was what I needed because the word that had instantly come to mind was *Lorax*, a tufted Dr. Seuss character. *"Thorax,"* I said. "And about the rest of it, if you could just chalk it up to early dementia I would be grateful."

Nick wrote in the word and seeing how nicely it fit, he smiled. My firstborn child had such a lovely smile it could be given out as a gift. "If you don't ask me whether or not I found a job today, I won't ask you if you're losing your mind."

"It's a deal," I said.

Then Nick put his cereal bowl on the floor, a few corn

flakes floating in a thin lake of milk, sending Red into a frantic, lapping ecstasy. Everybody was happy.

I remember so many details about that last day, the time I wasted answering e-mails, the two loads of laundry I folded and put away. Nick went off to his coffee shop, where he assumed his daily post scouring the Internet for job listings, and I changed his sheets and picked up towels off the floor because I was feeling like I owed him. Evie called to say she needed sixty dollars to replace the tiny underpants to her Ohio State cheerleading uniform, which had been lost, and I didn't have the nerve to ask her how they had been lost or how an article of clothing so insubstantial could be so expensive. I put the check in the mail. I wrote my weekly gardening column for the newspaper: "Your Chrysanthemums' Second Act." *Just because those bright yellow daisy mums have ceased their dazzling bloom, it doesn't mean they're bound for the compost heap.* Everything the same, everything in order, except that a couple of times I pulled down my sock to make sure my ankle was still there. By the end of the day I had come full circle and was back to thinking it had all been some crazy misunderstanding with the mirror.

Which was not to say I wasn't anxious for Arthur to come home and give me some plausible explanation for what had happened, or what it might have been had an eight-year-old been involved. Arthur and I had known each other since college, and even though I often found myself thinking we should find a way to spend a little more time together, I also thought of him as the person who knew me best in all the world, the person I was closest to.

I finished making dinner and left it in the oven to keep warm. I gave Red his dinner and then I took him for a walk. I poured a glass of wine. I started to read a book on composting because my next article was on composting. Nick came in briefly and went out again. I tried Arthur's cell phone. I read another chapter on composting.

Even for Arthur, 8:15 was late, and very late without a phone call. The chicken by now would be tough and dry, the fresh roasted asparagus reduced to the consistency of canned. I had become a fairly lousy cook over the years trying to guess the time of my husband's arrival. When we heard the back door open, Red and I sprang up and raced toward it, Red beating me there by three terrier lengths.

Arthur held up the palm of his hand. "Don't," he said. I stopped in my tracks but the dog did not. Arthur crouched down and scratched his ears. "I've got to take a shower. One of the Abbot girls threw up on me first thing this morning. I changed lab coats but I'm still feeling a little toxic. The nurses swore up and down that I smelled fine."

"Oh," I said. "Sure."

Arthur looked at Red. "I could fall over and go to sleep right here," he said, holding his muzzle. "Right on top of you."

"Do you want dinner?"

Arthur got up slowly, shaking his head no. "Sure," he

said. "Just let me clean up. You wouldn't believe all the things that happened today. A woman came in with trip-lets. All three of them had the croup. Then the head of the hospital board comes in and wants to talk to me about a new chief of staff and he stays for an hour, telling me one of his granddaughters bites her fingernails and his daughter is worried that the child may have some kind of mental dysfunction because of it and he's going on and on and it's two o'clock and I haven't finished seeing the morn-ing patients yet." He put his hand over his eyes and shook his head. "Sometimes I wonder how much longer I can do this."

"I wonder that myself," I said.

Arthur walked past me, keeping a safe distance. "Any news for Nick on the job front?"

"Not that he told me." Suddenly I felt unnerved, think-ing of what Gilda had said. *Is it Arthur?* When in the world was I supposed to work in the news of my day?

Arthur started up the stairs and then stopped halfway and called down over his shoulder. "Mary said you called today."

"I did," I said. I was looking at my hands, first the palm side and then the back. Still here.

"Any problems?"

I turned my face toward the stairs. I was going to say no, none at all, but he was already gone.

.   .   .

I had studied journalism and literature while Arthur was in medical school. I got that lousy job kids get at newspapers when I first started out, covering the city council meetings and the police desk from midnight to six a.m. But I was a reporter at heart and I always found something to report on. The great payola scandal in the state house of representatives? That was my story. I chased down labor bosses. I made myself a little name. After the kids were born I moved over to the arts section because the arts just seemed safer, and later I was editor of the book review section, because back then such things existed even in Ohio. For a long time I was very busy, reading and writing and assigning and editing and raising Nick and Evie. Arthur was building a practice and there were nights he got home before I did and he made dinner and left it warming in the oven for me, though even as I write that sentence I can scarcely believe it was true. It was right around that time that everything began to unspool and my whole career was played out in reverse. The Internet, that voracious weed, started to put the squeeze on us. The paper lost advertisers, the paper got smaller, the book review section became two pages, which became the occasional book review that I still write. By then no one thought I could be a reporter again, not even me. News could go to the arts but the arts never came back to news. I felt lucky to get the gardening column two days a week, especially because for the most part I was making it up as I went along. For every hour that was taken out of my job, another hour was added onto Arthur's. Maybe we were lucky. We had two kids, we needed the money. It was good that his practice was booming. With my newfound free time I drove the kids to soccer practice and ran the coat drive for the homeless and made better dinners, which would, over time, become worse dinners. It all worked out. It just didn't work out the way I thought it was going to.

I waited for a long time after the shower stopped running for Arthur to come back downstairs. When I finally went up I found him asleep on top of the bedspread wearing my toweling robe. His must have been in the wash. I got a blanket out of the closet and covered him up. I never even considered waking him to tell him what had happened. He was exhausted, he needed to sleep. It was a decision I later came to regret. By the next morning I was gone.

two

I think I knew it as soon as I woke up, maybe even in the moment before I opened my eyes. It could have been that I was dreaming I was invisible, people bumping into me at a cocktail party, stepping on my toes. When I stuck my hand out from underneath the covers and saw nothing I hardly even felt surprised. If anything I was vindicated. It wasn't my imagination! Looking down, I could see the shape of myself beneath the blankets. It was just a shorter version of the shape that Arthur made beside me, the only difference

being that there was a head on Arthur's pillow. At the foot
of the bed Red made a neat ball between us. It wasn't that
I had been reduced to nothing exactly, had that been the
case the bed would have appeared to contain only a man
and a dog, it's that I had been reduced to something mys-
tifyingly clear—definite substance and no form. I thought
about waking up Arthur but considering yesterday's debacle
with Nick I decided to just wait until I came back. After I
was visible again I'd figure out what was going on.

And so I waited, my invisible arms behind my invisible
head. Of course, I didn't know exactly when I'd vanished
yesterday. Could it have been in the shower? Was it possible that I could have washed my hair without realizing I
was gone? And then something else occurred to me, something darker and more unsettling: what if yesterday wasn't
the first time? What if I had been flickering in and out for a
while now—in my sleep or in the car or in the kitchen chop-
ping vegetables? It had been years since I'd really kept an
eye on myself. Could I be positive how long this had been
going on?

My need to look in the mirror was becoming overwhelm-
ing. As quietly as possible, I rolled out of bed and stepped
into my slippers. My nightgown came down well past my
knees with sleeves past my elbows, and even though there
was nothing sexy about it, it had a pretty scoop neckline and
was soft from years of washing. It had once been pink but

now was more a color that called pink to mind. I stood in front of the mirror on the back of the closet door and looked at the nightgown floating there, the slippers standing empty. I tried to remain calm. I would come back. It was only a matter of waiting it out.

"You're up early," Arthur said in a sleepy voice.

I jumped. The nightgown jumped. And then I turned around. *For better or for worse,* I thought. *In sickness and in health.* "Arthur?"

"I fell asleep on you last night," he said. "I'm so sorry. I got out of the shower and thought I could lie down for one minute. I used to be able to do that when I was an intern. Remember the one-minute nap?" He sighed, stretched. "I'm not the man I used to be, Clover." He patted the bedspread beside him and Red wiggled up and rolled over on his back, presenting his tummy. "I'm a dog," Arthur said, giving Red a vigorous scratch. "We're both dogs, aren't we, Red?"

"Hey," I said, not thinking there was any need to state the obvious.

"That reminds me." He closed his eyes and pressed a palm to his forehead. "There's a group meeting tonight and the drug reps are bringing in dinner so count me as covered."

"What reminds you?"

"What?"

"You said 'that reminds me.'"

"No," he said, shaking his head. "Nothing reminded me. I'm just free associating. It's so nice to just have a minute to talk. Did I tell you Missy Tate came in with her baby

yesterday as a new patient? Missy was one of my first patients. She was two years old when her parents brought her
in. She had been one of Jack Aldo's patients when he re-
tired. You remember Jack Aldo, I got a lot of his practice.
Anyway, the prettiest little girl. As soon as she walked in the
door I knew who she was, and she had her baby who looked
just like her. God, tell me that didn't make me feel like I was
one hundred and ten."

"You knew her on sight," I said. "Pretty amazing." Here's
an interesting fact: I was neither warm nor cold. Invisibility seemed to exist at a perfectly controlled temperature. I
smoothed down the front of my nightgown with my hands.
I cleared my throat.

"Could you do me a huge favor?" Arthur asked. He was
sitting halfway up in bed now, still wearing my robe. It
would appear he was looking right at me but who's to say?
He didn't have his glasses on and the room was not especially light.

"Name it." What if I wasn't gone, or I was only gone to
myself? That would mean that this was insanity. Insanity
being two rungs below invisibility on the ladder of diseases
I wished to be suffering from.

"Would you make me a big breakfast? Eggs and bacon,
the works? I'm starving."

"You didn't have dinner."

"Right." He cocked a finger at me. "I didn't have dinner
and I probably won't have lunch today and who knows what
the drug reps will bring for dinner, so this is my best bet

for a meal today." Then he got out of bed, and coming right toward me, he patted the small of my back and went into the bathroom. "You're the best," Arthur said, and then he closed the door behind him.

It turns out I was not invisible after all. That left partial blindness and mental illness. I made the bed and got dressed—jeans and a sweater and socks and shoes. I pulled out a hat and scarf and gloves to walk Red. Maybe I didn't need them but I put them on anyway. Once I was dressed I looked remarkably like myself, an absent version of myself but it was better than nothing, which is what I had started with. Red followed me out to get the paper and down to the end of the block and back. I saw no one and no one saw me. Back in the kitchen I took off the hat and gloves because if this was mental illness, wearing a hat and gloves to make breakfast would look even crazier. I found the end of a goat cheese log in the refrigerator, the last decent tomato, some basil. I got out the bacon and the bread. The whole time I was thinking, I may be out of my mind but at least I can still make a nice breakfast. I poured out juice and coffee. I put a little pitcher of milk beside the cup, an unnecessarily attentive flourish. The bacon was spattering away in the pan, the eggs firmed up nicely. Cue the husband, handsome in his suit, walking into the kitchen, a tie in each hand.

"Which one?" he asked.

"The blue whales." Arthur's taste in ties ran toward the whimsical. The knife worked up and down, seemingly by itself, over the tender skin of the tomato and then across the basil, making a chiffonade.

Arthur sat down and folded the arts section to the crossword puzzle. I had put a pencil next to his fork. I had thought of everything. "What a lucky guy I am," he said when I set down the plate, but he wasn't looking at the plate, or the absence of the hand that left it on the place mat. He was looking at the paper. Red was looking up at Arthur, mesmerized by the smell of bacon.

"What are we going to do about Nick?" Arthur said absently, the folded puzzle in one hand, fork in the other.

What are we going to do about Nick? For the first time I realized that it wasn't a question. It was a conversational filler, like asking what the weather was going to do. It was the thing we said to each other when there wasn't anything to say. "Another piece of toast?" I answered by way of experiment.

Arthur looked at his watch and in response took a long, fast drink of coffee. "No, no. I've got patients starting at seven thirty. I have to go. It was a great breakfast." He stopped then, checked the paper one more time. "What's that Melville novel? The short one?"

"Omoo," I said. It seemed like it was in the puzzle once a week. He never remembered it.

He bit off half a piece of bacon and gave the other half to Red, then he wrote in the answer. "You're a genius," he said. "By the way, I left that suit on the floor in the closet, the one the kid threw up on. If you're out today—"

"Right to the dry cleaners."

That was when my husband blew a kiss in my direction and was out the door.

The toast was gone, the bacon, the coffee, the juice, but that perfect little goat cheese omelet sat on the plate untouched. I picked up Arthur's fork and took a bite. For a minute I thought about running out to the garage and telling him to come back. It was that good. It was also wasted on me because I really didn't have much of an appetite. I took a couple of bites and pushed the plate away.

After I cleaned up the kitchen, I put the hat and gloves back on and took Red over to Gilda's. She had a glass front door, which was something I could never figure out, and she waved to me as she walked across her front hallway and I waved back to her. Red started barking like crazy, hopping up and down. Red was nuts about Gilda.

I pulled off my gloves and hat when she opened the door. Red shot in like a bullet and started jumping all over her. Suddenly I felt like crying. "You were right," I said. "I've lost my mind."

Gilda crouched down to rub the dog and when she looked up to ask me what I was talking about all of the color drained from her face. She covered her mouth with her hands.

"What?" I said. Honestly for a second I wasn't putting it all together. It had been a very confusing morning.

"What do you mean, *what?* I can't see you."

I held out my hands in front of me and my hands weren't there and all of a sudden it hit me—I had in fact disappeared and my husband had failed to notice. "I thought I was crazy!" I sat down next to her in the front hall and put my head between my knees. I felt like I was going to faint.

I wondered what it meant to have low blood pressure when you didn't have any blood.

"Didn't you notice?" Gilda's voice was shrill. She wasn't screaming exactly but her tone was piercing.

"I was sure that Arthur saw me. I kept trying to talk to him about it but he didn't seem to think anything was wrong. I woke Nick up yesterday and asked him if I was invisible and he acted like I was a complete idiot because by then I wasn't invisible, except maybe I was still invisible and he just didn't notice." Now I had started to cry. I could feel the big wet tears running down my face. I could see them hitting my pants and making dark spots. "I didn't want to go through all that with Arthur. I mean, you'd say something if you noticed your wife wasn't there but she was still talking to you, wouldn't you?"

"Clovie, this is serious." She leaned forward and with one tentative finger pulled down the front of my sweater. "You're completely gone."

"He didn't notice!" A pure grief washed through me. It was bigger than the problem at hand.

"Do you need a Kleenex? I can't tell."

A fresh sob burst forward and I nodded my head.

"Can I get you some Kleenex?" she said.

Head nodding was out. I tried to catch my breath. "Please," I said.

Gilda scrambled to her feet and Red made his way into my lap. I ran my invisible hand over his head and down his back, watching as his fur flattened out and then sprung up again. It was hypnotic, really, the mechanics of petting.

"Were you invisible when he came home last night?" Gilda put the Kleenex box on the floor in front of me and sat down, though not too close.

I took a tissue and dried my eyes, blew my nose. I was certainly generating fluid. "I have to think. Everything is jumbled in my head now." Arthur was late. Arthur was coming in the door. "No, I was still here last night. He was completely exhausted. He fell asleep before dinner."

"Are you *sure* you were there?"

I nodded, then checked myself. "I think I'm sure, not that it makes any difference."

"It does make a difference. You're going to have to tell someone. You at least have to go to the doctor. Clearly there is something very wrong with you."

"I'll go to the doctor as soon as I come back," I said, though in truth I couldn't think of the last time I went to the doctor. I got Jeannine, Arthur's nicest nurse, to call in the refills for my prescriptions. I felt like not going to the doctor was the perk of being married to a doctor.

"When you come back from where? Don't tell me you're planning on going somewhere like this?"

"I just meant when I come back, you know, when you can see me again."

"But what if you don't come back?" Gilda extended her hand as if she had meant to take mine and then she thought better of it. "What makes you think this is something that just goes away?"

"I came back yesterday," I said defensively. I found

myself petting Red faster and suddenly Gilda was watching his fur go up and down and I stopped.

"This is uncharted territory. You have no idea how long you're going to stay this way. How long were you invisible yesterday?"

"Maybe fifteen minutes."

"And what about today?"

I leaned over to look at Gilda's watch. "I don't know actually. This is how I woke up."

"So let's say you became invisible just after you went to sleep. You could have been like this up to eight or ten hours by now."

"Will you *stop*?" I stood up from the floor. "You're not making me feel any better."

"I'm not trying to make you feel better. I'm telling you, you need to get to a doctor. You probably should go to the emergency room. I can drive you."

That was when Benny stuck his head around the corner. He was six foot three and looked as much like a skeleton as any boy who had found himself tall overnight ever did. "Mom, are you taking me to school or what?"

"You don't say hello anymore?" Gilda said.

"Hi, Mrs. Hobart. Hi, Red. We're already late."

Red jumped off my lap and ran over to say hello to Benny. We both looked up at him as if we'd been caught doing something we shouldn't have been doing. The boy was nothing but angles, all elbows and knees. Even his hair was sticking out in starched planes.

"I'll be right there," Gilda said. "My keys are in my purse. Go start the car."

"Bye, Mrs. Hobart," Benny said, and gave me a little wave. He went around the corner and then just as quickly came back. "Why are you guys on the floor?"

"Red had something stuck in his paw," Gilda said, deftly dispatching one of the innumerable lies of motherhood. "Now give me one minute."

We waited until we heard the back door close and then we looked at each other, which is to say I looked at Gilda and she looked at the top of my sweater. "I'm still not here, right?" I said.

"Maybe men can see you and women can't."

"I'm sitting here, a sweater, a pair of pants, no head, no hands. He just didn't notice?"

"No," she said sadly. "He didn't."

"Okay." I got up off the floor. "I'm going to go call the doctor."

"I can drive you over as soon as I get back."

"I still know how to drive. I'll wear some glasses and a hat. The one thing we can be sure of is that nobody's going to notice."

It turns out I hadn't been to the doctor in even longer than I'd thought because when I called Dr. Perkins's office, I was told that he had moved to Minneapolis two years ago. His practice had been divided among the other doctors, the nurse informed me, and it was my lucky day because Dr. Anderson had a cancellation at eleven. What kind of insurance did I have?

I hesitated. There was no such thing as an internist who was available to see you on the very day you wanted to go. I knew I should call Arthur, who could at least tell me whether or not he'd heard of Dr. Anderson, but Arthur would never call me back because Mary wouldn't give him the message until the end of the day, and if for some reason he did call me back he would want to know if I was sick, and I would no doubt say something along the lines of *as if you'd ever notice*. And that wouldn't be a good place to start the conversation.

"Ma'am?" the nurse said. "Do you want to take the appointment?"

I did.

I had a memory of an old black-and-white movie about an invisible man that I had seen on television as a child. I think it was supposed to be scary, though I don't remember anything particularly scary about it. What I remember was that when the invisible man needed to be seen he wrapped himself up in an endless strip of surgical gauze and put on a suit and a hat and dark glasses. When he needed to disappear, he simply twirled down to nothing, stepping out of the pile of clothing and gauze to get away scot-free. I, on the other hand, having taken the most limited of surveys, didn't think this was going to be my problem. I suppose I ran the risk of alarming someone but there was no chance they were going to be more alarmed than I was. I simply dressed to achieve maximum coverage, which was appropriate for the weather, and then I added on glasses and a hat.

Dr. Caleb Anderson was in a practice of ten internists, of which he was the alphabetical front man. I went through the transaction at the receptionist's desk with complete ease: I signed in, handed over my insurance card, filled out a ream of paperwork regarding my medical history, my ability to pay, and how I was feeling today, then I sat in a corner behind a magazine and waited.

"Clover Hobart?" called a heavyset young woman in flowered scrubs. She was looking at my chart as I followed her through the door and down the hallway. "How are you feeling today?" she asked over her shoulder.

"Invisible," I said.

"Don't you hate that?" She patted the scale. "Hop on up here for me."

I stepped up. For the first time in my life I was sincerely curious. For all I knew I didn't weigh any more than my clothes. The girl pushed the iron weights up and then gently tapped them back down.

"One hundred forty-two," she said.

"Really?" I leaned forward to look for myself but she quickly slid the weights down to the end as if to erase the evidence.

"I won't listen to any complaints about one forty-two. I would kill to weigh one forty-two." We sat down at a desk, where she took my blood pressure without making me roll up the sleeve of my long-sleeved T-shirt, took my temperature by handing me the thermometer, and asked me questions about my medications and alcohol consumption, whose answers she dutifully recorded in my chart. When all of that was through, she put me in a room and told me to wait. "The doctor is going to be right with you," she said.

Maybe being invisible wasn't a problem. It was depressing to find out just how little attention people paid, but I was beginning to think there would probably be some advantages. For one thing, I would never worry about that crease between my eyebrows again.

"Clover?" The door was open and I looked up to see a young man in a white coat holding my chart.

"Yes?"

"I'm Dr. Anderson." He put the chart down next to the sink and started to wash his hands, a task he performed in a manner that would have made Howard Hughes blush. "I see you were a patient of Dr. Perkins."

"I was."

"Well, we all miss Bill but he's doing great up in Minnesota. Both of his daughters live in Minnesota." He was working over the left hand with a little brush, employing such vigor that I had to wonder what exactly he had been doing in the room before mine.

"I didn't know that."

"He said it was the fishing that got him up there but I don't know that those girls didn't have something to do with it." He switched the brush to his left hand and then began to dig into the right. He looked over at the open file beside him. "It says the last time you were in was more than three years ago. It says you had some arthritis in your left shoulder and Dr. Perkins sent you to a rheumatologist, Dr. Sewa. Did you like Dr. Sewa?"

I strained to remember. It was a long time ago, and I don't think I had been in his presence for more than three minutes. "I did," I said, mostly to be polite. "It turned out to be tendonitis."

Dr. Anderson was now washing his wrists, using his fore-arm to pump liquid soap onto one wrist and then grind-ing them together in a circular motion so as not to involve his already clean hands. Hand washing, it seemed to me, should be like stair sweeping—you start at the highest point and work your way down. I did not mention this. "That's good!" he said brightly. "You don't want to get arthritis at your age. Really, not at any age." He finished up with the soap and then just held his wrists under the water for a long, long time. From where I was sitting they looked raw. "So it says here you're doing some hormone replacement therapy and taking Ostafoss for calcium."

"I am." I didn't mention the antidepressant, Singsall. It was such a little dose, a pinch. Arthur had talked me into trying it when, two years after the book review section folded in our paper, I would still get weepy on Sundays when I saw the *New York Times Book Review.* I was sure I could go off it now but the truth was I liked it. It just brightened things up a bit, made the day run smoother. I never saw any reason to tell Dr. Perkins about it and I saw even less reason to tell Dr. Anderson. In fact, I realized now, I didn't want to tell Dr. Anderson anything. He had been in the room for five minutes. If he hadn't noticed that there was no one sitting in these clothes, then he wasn't the man for the job.

"I'll tell you, I think you should go off the Premacore. It puts you at an increased risk of breast cancer."

"I've taken that into account." Though what I wanted to suggest was that he should try going through menopause sometime and get back to me.

He dried his hands on seventeen paper towels. Seventeen actual towels. I counted as he pulled them out of the wall dispenser. "After we get some blood work we'll sit down and discuss it, figure out what's best for you." He took a pen out of his coat pocket. I was surprised that he didn't even bother to rinse it off. He made a couple of check marks on my chart. "Do you wear a seat belt, Clover?"

I looked up at him, or at his back. "Are you serious?"

"It's good to ask. People forget."

"But what about why I came in today? Shouldn't you ask about that first?"

"Is that shoulder still bothering you?" He circled his own shoulder as if the very question had made it tight.

"I'm invisible," I said. I sat there waiting. I didn't want to get into it with him but at the same time it was impossible to not even mention it.

He nodded his head. "You wouldn't believe how often I hear that. Once we get that blood work done we'll know what's missing. Don't worry about it for now. We'll get you fixed up. If you wait here just another minute, Polly will take you down to the lab."

I thought about offering my hand, but considering how clean his hands were, coupled with the fact that he'd never so much as taken my pulse, I felt it would be kinder not to. I waited a minute after the door closed before I picked up my purse and left. No one tried to stop me on the way out. It was possible they didn't see me.

three

After that, I'll admit it, I was low. I didn't come back the way I thought I would, or not so much. One afternoon I was my same old self from the knees down for more than three hours. I quickly clipped my toenails and shaved my legs, though once those legs were gone again I had to wonder why I'd bothered. Sometimes I would catch sight of my own hand reaching across the table, the odd elbow, but these encounters with myself were always fleeting. As for Arthur and Nick, I'd made a terrible mistake. Instead of telling them what had happened, I dared them not to notice for themselves.

And they didn't notice.

I continued to fix the food and clean the house without them having the slightest clue as to what was missing. I made a small effort to participate in conversation, but more and more I withdrew. In time, I didn't come and sit with them at dinner, and when Arthur asked if I was feeling all right I only said I'd read in Oprah's magazine that it was better to not eat after five. This feeble ploy struck them as completely reasonable.

There were so many extra hours in the day! Had I really spent that much of my time on personal grooming? On small exchanges with the postman when he came to deliver the mail? Now I dressed for maximum coverage without any thought as to how I looked. No one cared how I looked. No one saw. I felt like I was under quarantine, except that I could go wherever I liked. I picked up Arthur's suit from the cleaners, I went to the grocery store. Sometimes someone would notice that something was off and it was always a young girl who wouldn't allow herself to believe what her eyes were telling her and so she'd look quickly away, embarrassed, the way she might have if I'd had one eye in the center of my forehead. It was obvious her mother had drilled a lifetime of good manners into her. *It isn't polite to stare.* But I always wanted to say to the girl, stare all you want, there's nothing here to see.

"Maybe you should go to a therapist," Gilda said.

I sighed. "And when the therapist failed to notice I wasn't there I'd only get more depressed."

"You have to start taking some responsibility for your circumstances," she said. "It's been over a week now. You're not a newbie anymore." Gilda, mother of five, was a true believer in tough love.

"What do you suggest I do? Have Red trained as a service animal?" I was running a dust mop around Gilda's kitchen floor while we were talking. Cleaning was my attempt to find some order in the world.

"Well, for one thing, you could talk to your husband before I do."

The mop came to an abrupt halt. "Don't you dare."

"It's bad enough that you're invisible," Gilda said. "But watching you play these unnecessary games with Arthur is getting to be unbearable."

"You think Steve would notice if you were missing, don't you? Why don't you just go ahead and say it?"

That was when Benny and his older brother Miller came into the room. Each of them took a banana out of the fruit bowl. "Hi, Mrs. Hobart," they said in unison.

"Hey, guys," I said.

"Mom," Benny said. "Miller said he'd drive me over to the comic book store."

"Is Nick home?" Miller asked me, leaning over to pet Red.

"I don't know where he is," I said. "Why don't you call his cell? I know he'd want to go."

"Cool," Miller said, and then he looked at me. "Mrs. Hobart?"

"Yes?"

"Why are you cleaning our house?"

"Because I finished cleaning mine," I said flatly, and steered the mop toward the dining room.

Once the boys had left, Gilda came and put her hand lightly on my back. "You can't take it personally. We're just not interesting to them," she said.

"I don't care that I'm not interesting to your family, but I do mean to be interesting to my own family."

"You are. They love you more than anything. They just take you for granted, that's all. If anything ever happened to you they'd be devastated."

"Something *did* happen to me." I stopped and wiped the sleeve of my sweater over my eyes.

"You should at least go and see another doctor. There's got to be a specialist."

"An invisibility specialist?" I sniffed. "I don't think so."

"What if you called your brother?"

"If Arthur's too busy to figure out what's going on with me, then George doesn't stand a chance." My younger brother had married at fifty, invested in Clomid, and immediately had a set of gorgeous twin girls with his forty-five-year-old dermatologist wife. He was sunk.

"But isn't he an endocrinologist? Don't you think invisibility would be related to the endocrine system?"

"If I get diabetes on top of everything else I'll be sure to call him. Listen, I know you're trying to help me but I really think I'm beyond help. I need to figure out how to come to terms with this because I don't think anybody's going to fix it." With that I went outside and shook out the mop, then I stood for a minute and watched the endless dust motes falling like a silvered snow in the autumn light. Even the dust was more identifiable than I was.

When I went home I checked my cell phone and found a text message from my daughter.

R U D-PRESSED?

If I was depressed, wouldn't it be nicer to call? And what was with the dash? Didn't it take as much time to type a dash as it would have taken to type an *e*? Texting was the heartbreak of all English majors.

WHO TOLD YOU I WAS DEPRESSED?

I held the phone and waited. It was my belief that Evie took her showers with her cell phone in one hand. I imagined her executing her perilous cheerleading flips while texting. One day she would text through her own wedding. I could call her and not hear back for a week, but sending a text meant a guaranteed reply in under five seconds. She must have come to some kind of understanding with her teachers.

DAD.

I nodded my head. At least he noticed something was different.

I'M FINE. DON'T WORRY.

And I suppose she didn't, because that was the last I heard from her.

I ran out of things to do so early in the day. I had already written a listless column on spring bulbs, "An Act of Faith in Your Own Backyard."

> No one knows what the future holds. We think we have a long life ahead of us and then bang, the guy barreling toward the intersection never sees the light turn red. Still, nothing says "I believe in tomorrow" like the willingness to spend a back-breaking afternoon chipping holes into the frozen earth and dropping in a handful of fancy Dutch tulip bulbs. Will the voles eat them before they ever have the chance to take root? Were the bulbs actually twenty years old and the joke was on you for buying them in the first place? Will you wind up with an armload of bright red tulips the size of goose eggs that would make Martha Stewart weep with envy? You'll just have to wait until spring to find out.

When I sent it in I got a one word e-mail back from my editor, Ed. DEPRESSED?

At least he'd bothered to use the *e*.

I decided I would go to the grocery store and then take

Red to the park. Red, the only mammal in my life who still seemed able to see me, was pretty much my main companion these days. I pushed my cart listlessly up and down the aisles. Nothing sounded good to me and I could no longer make myself care what Nick and Arthur liked to eat. I picked up bags of rice and cans of beans and frozen trays of macaroni and cheese, food for the apocalypse. My mood was not improved by the fact that the checkout girl and the bagging boy were locked in a rapturous flirtation and never unlocked their eyes from each other the entire time I dropped my supplies on the electronic conveyor belt. I lugged the groceries out to the car and Red and I started out of the parking lot. That was when I saw a man, a big man, leaning over a woman who was considerably smaller and pressed into the side of a car. His face was bent down near her face and he was yelling at her. Though my windows were up and I couldn't make out the words, I could get the general gist from their faces—he was furious, she was frightened. At any other time in my life I would have driven by. I would have thought, *bastard,* or *poor girl,* but today I stopped the car. Today my thought was *Mister, I have had enough of you.* I left the keys in the ignition, closing the door so that Red wouldn't follow me, and I walked up to the trouble at hand. "Do you need help here?" I asked the woman.

The man told me to mind my own business, though he didn't say it nicely. I could smell his sweat, his beery breath. I could see the tails of his tattoos poking out from the cuffs of his winter jacket. So where was my fear? I did not have a drop in me. For the first time this difference in myself didn't feel like such a bad thing. I felt clear as in pure, clear-headed, a force of determination.

"Do you need help here?" I said again. I went to stand beside the woman. She was smaller than I was and I put my hand on her arm.

"It's okay," she said to me, but her tone was unconvincing.

"Tell her to get lost!" the man said to the woman he had pinned. He wasn't that old, really, probably not even thirty. He had a beard and mustache that looked as if they had been drawn in with an eyebrow pencil. I was so close to his face I could see the inordinate amount of time it must have taken him to shave. I could see that the gold hoop in his ear contained the tiniest diamond chip known to man and still the sun managed to catch it for a second and make a flash.

I pulled off my glove and put my hand on his chest. I pushed him back. I don't mean to say I had superhuman strength, but very ordinary strength, when applied to some-one who was in no way expecting it, is more powerful than you would think. It didn't take much to put myself between him and the woman, and when I was between them I used my free hand to take off my hat. "Look at me!" I said, be-cause even as I was getting in his face he had not thought to look at mine. He was in essence looking through my head and into the face of the young woman behind me, and I continued to push him back until he figured out there were somehow three of us there, and that was enough to pull the glue out of his seams. I put my hands on either side of his face and brought his head toward me so that he would feel my breath in his ear. "I will follow you every minute of your life," I said. "I will be with you all the time. Do you understand me? Bother this woman again, bother any of us, and I will be on you so fast you'll never see it coming."

He took several steps back, at which point the woman scrambled into the car and locked the doors. That's when I noticed there was a baby seat in the car with a strapped-in toddler who was just starting to cry.

I patted his shoulder. "Okay," I said. "Get out of here."

He flailed his arms around like something was crawling on him but I just stepped aside. The woman was backing up fast and she clipped the bumper of my car as she spun out and away. The man with the fine-line beard watched her go, and while he was watching her I got in my car.

I was shaking! Shaking! And not because I was scared. In fact, I realized I had been scared all week and for the first time that feeling had passed. What had replaced it was the force of life pulsing through me. I had made him see me! I had made him listen! I suddenly was overcome with a desire to fight crime. Is this how it happens? Do people drive around town looking for kidnappings and armed robberies to bust up?

Red and I got out at the park and I put him on the leash and together we ran a victory lap around the circumference. "The times they are a-changin'," I sang out loud, and then I said to Red, "Power to invisible people!"

. . .

Arthur got called in to the hospital just as he was leaving the office, a possible case of meningitis, and Nick had left a note saying he was going over to Miller's house to watch a ball game, so that left me and Red to have a bowl of popcorn for dinner and look at pay-per-view. We picked a comic-book action movie that touted an invisible woman, but what a load of hokum she turned out to be. She was about twenty-three years old with long blond curls, endless legs, and significant cleavage spilling out of her low-cut spandex unitard. She controlled her invisibility at will by closing her eyes, lowering her chin, and pursing her pretty lips together as if she were trying to solve a particularly difficult problem on an algebra exam. When she needed to be seen again, because such beauty was certainly a more powerful weapon than any superpower she could have wound up with, I suppose she just did the same thing in reverse and *poof!* she was back.

I turned it off halfway through, never even caring about whether or not the planet could be saved from evil masterminds. The premise was too ridiculous. To think a girl like that could ever be invisible.

I left a note on the table for Arthur telling him his dinner was all laid out on a plate in the fridge, and went to bed. I didn't know how much time had passed, and I didn't know whether I was awake or asleep, when Arthur crawled into bed beside me.

"Hey," I whispered, not wanting to wake the dog.

"Hey," he whispered back. He scooted up behind me and folded me in his arms. "My hands are cold."

"They're fine." I took his hands in my hands. It was a dark night, no moon through the window, and we lay there like this for a while, just holding each other like nothing had ever been wrong. "Hard day?" I asked.

"It was pretty much like the others, maybe a little bit longer. What about you?"

"It was better than the others," I said, and then I told him my story, a slightly modified version in which I was a little less brave and not at all invisible but still, the basic facts were true.

Arthur came up on his elbow and put his hand over my heart. "I can't believe you! You could have been hurt! You could have been killed! For all you knew that man had a gun."

"If he had a gun, then all the more reason to stop him. I did the right thing. You would have done it, too."

"I don't know," he said. "I'd like to think so but I don't know. What did the woman say to you once he left?"

"She didn't say a thing. She got in her car just as soon as I pushed him away and pulled out as fast as she could." I told him that the edge of my fender was slightly crushed and that I saw she had a child in the car.

"Clover, Clover, Clover," he said, and wrapped me up in his arms. "I'm trying to diagnose a lousy case of meningitis and you're out there saving the world."

"It had to be saved," I said. Then Arthur kissed me, and I kissed him.

To tell the truth, I made love with my eyes closed most

of the time. Arthur did, too. I knew because from time to time I'd opened my eyes and looked at the sweet intensity on his face. We've been doing this a long time, the two of us, ever since college, waiting for one of our roommates to go out for pizza so that we could bolt the door and fall against each other with all of our twenty-year-old passion. Year after month and week after day we have come back to each other. We would know each other's bodies blind. As for being invisible, I forgot about it that night, and Arthur never knew.

The next morning when he leaned in and kissed my shoulder, my neck, I started to think about it all another way. Maybe Arthur didn't see me because he knew me so well and his vision automatically filled in all the things I was, based on the slightest hint of shape or scent. Maybe when you've been with someone so long you don't so much see them as you project them onto things. Arthur could have been making love to my twenty-year-old self, my forty-year-old self. He could have made love to all the women I had ever been. Maybe he saw all of us together. Anyway, this morning I was willing to give him the benefit of the doubt. I made him breakfast, I wished him a good day. I sat down at the kitchen table and ate the piece of toast he hadn't had time for, then I picked up the local paper. My piece on composting was in: "This Year's Eggshells Are Next Year's Tomatoes." I started to read it through but it was too boring. I looked at the front page, which discussed the potential merits of a new ice-skating rink, the recipes ("Living Large with Quinoa"), my horoscope ("Today you will take a chance on a new group of friends who think that you'll fit right in with their club"). I looked at the puppies to good homes column. I asked Red if he was interested in having a friend. He wagged his tail and I realized he was interested in the rest of my toast so I gave it to him. My eyes scanned the want ads, apartments for rent, pianos for sale, men wanting women, men wanting men, calling invisible women.

I stopped. I went back. There, between a notice for a divorced Christian singles group and a notice for Tupperware representatives, was the following:

Calling Invisible Women.
Downtown Sheraton, Wednesday at 10:00 a.m.
Bring a Kleenex.

Was it possible that the answer was in our pitiful newspaper that I very nominally still worked for? I went to the computer and googled "Invisible Women," but all that came up were pictures of the blond girl in the superhero suit followed by a series of articles about women who loved too much and did too much and gave too much. I tried "Invisible Women Ohio" and "Calling Invisible Women" but

four

I was worrying about what I should wear. How dressy was a meeting of invisible women? Were there wigs involved? I had considered getting a wig, but the more time that went by the less imperative it felt. I put on black tights and boots, a plain dark dress with a collar that could be turned up. In truth, I thought I looked good. I had lost some weight since becoming invisible. Food was less interesting when no one could see you eat it. I took off my clothes and put on a skirt and a sweater but it lacked sophistication. It said, I'm a preppy housewife who thinks being invisible is fun! Not the message I wanted to send. I tried a nice pair of jeans and a blazer but then what if they thought I didn't care? I went back to the dress and added on the scarf that Arthur had bought me for our anniversary last year. I kept telling myself that I was getting all worked up for nothing. This was not going to be a group of women who were invisible, this was going to be a couple of plastic surgeons peddling the joys of facial fillers. This was going to be the first meeting of a new Weight Watchers club. This was going to be another encounter with the metaphor of invisibility because as far as the real thing was concerned, I seemed to be the only one suffering from that. Still, how could I not go? It wasn't every day a call for invisible women was going to run in the paper.

When I went downstairs, Nick was in the kitchen eating breakfast. He glanced up, giving me a split second of his morning's attention. "Where are you going?"

"What makes you think I'm going anywhere?"

"You're not wearing sweatpants."

I poured myself a cup of coffee and refilled his. "I have to go in to the paper. Every now and then we have to check in with the mother ship."

"Crappy paper," Nick said, sliding it in my direction. It was still perfectly folded. He was reading the *Times*.

"True," I sighed, and nodded my head. "But it used to pay the bills."

"That must have been nice," Nick said. "Think up something you're actually interested in doing, something you might be good at, and then go to that place and get a job and then they train you and over time you learn to take on more responsibility and you get better at it. I want to live in a world where I could at least think, 'There's a newspaper! Maybe I can write for a newspaper!'"

"The job search isn't going so well?"

I watched Nick's shoulders slump forward, a nearly imperceptible bend. "I appreciate how rarely you ask about it. It shows real discipline on your part. Dad, on the other hand, thinks that maybe I'm performing neurosurgery somewhere and just forgot to mention it. I keep telling him, once I get a job the two of you will be the first to know. I'm actually doing the crossword puzzle just to spite him. I figured out he was hiding them in the knife drawer."

"I can pick up another paper," I said.

"I just wish I knew what I was supposed to be doing. I'm overqualified for every job that's stupid and underqualified for every job that's smart."

"I know how you feel."

It was the moment when a different son might have looked his mother in the eye, but my son pressed down his chin and studied the paper harder. "How do you know how I feel?"

Because, my love, you feel invisible. You think you have no definition. "Well, I used to have a demanding full-time job," I said, because this was also true. "I used to have a career. I'm a little underemployed myself at the moment."

"But you're a mom," he said, letting himself sound younger

than he was. "You've got a house and a dog and you're married to a doctor. You're fine."

"It's not all about the money, kiddo. You're right, I'm not out on the street, but neither are you." I squeezed his wrist. "I bet we'll both find something."

"You've got a meeting," he said, brushing me off. "Underemployed people shouldn't be late for meetings."

"Okay," I said. "You're right. Throw the tennis ball for Red a few times before you go?"

"Sure," he said. "I'm good at that. If there was a job posting for a tennis-ball thrower for terriers I'd have it all sewn up." He filled in another word. "Oh, by the way, Grandma called. Maybe you were in the shower. She wanted to know why you haven't been in yoga class. She said that Dad told her you were depressed."

"Dad has apparently been handing out leaflets to that effect."

"So I told her that was crazy and I'd never seen you so happy in my life. I said you were probably missing yoga because you've been raising money to cure cancer and hanging out with your friends and writing great articles and teaching Red to balance on a beach ball."

"Did you tell her that?"

Nick was quiet for a moment. "Yeah. I did."

Arthur's mother taught yoga at the YMCA on Tuesday and Thursday mornings and weekly meditation workshops at the Unitarian Church on Saturday afternoons and the occasional vegetarian cooking class, though now she was a vegan. She was seventy-six. She would be sympathetic to my invisibility. She would also be positive that she knew exactly how to reverse it, and that would no doubt involve me drinking great quantities of wheatgrass juice. I just wasn't feeling up to wheatgrass yet. I told my son I loved him and went out to face the unknown.

Over the years I had attended many of my children's sports banquets at the Sheraton (that's counting cheerleading as a sport), along with a few bridal shows and a couple of Ohio board of tourism conventions that I covered for the paper. So it wasn't as if I had any problems walking into the Sheraton, but still, it was taking me a few minutes to get my courage up. I sat in the car until 9:50 and then took out the fresh Kleenex I had put in the side pocket of my purse and went inside.

For a few minutes I snooped around discreetly, looking for an easel with a signboard on it saying "Welcome, Invisible Women!" or something like that. When I didn't find anything, I went to the front desk, where a dark-haired girl in a navy suit was typing away at a computer. "Excuse me," I said.

"Just one minute," she said, drawing the word *one* out until it had five syllables. She didn't look up and so I was left to stand there and admire the gloss of her hair, wondering how it was that girls who worked in hotels always had such glossy hair, when I suddenly felt a strong hand on my upper arm, a security guard's grip that was steering me away.

"Hey!" I said sharply.

The glossy-haired girl, no doubt thinking I was reprimanding her for having asked me to wait, glanced up just in time to see me being dragged across the lobby by nothing at all.

"One minute," a quiet voice said.

I was marched around the corner to a row of comfortable chairs and was then deposited into one of those chairs. The grip on my arm was released, and the chair beside me turned in my direction.

"Sorry about that," the voice said. "I'm always telling the group we should put more information in the ad."

"I was just going to ask where the meeting was." I spoke to the air.

"The people at the Sheraton don't know we use their hotel. The old-timers get here early to grab up the newcomers but I was in the bathroom. My bad."

"Excuse me?" There was absolutely nothing there, but then I saw it, crumpled in the corner of the chair, a Kleenex. Was this really possible? I reached into my pocket and pulled out a Kleenex of my own.

"I know you're invisible," the voice said. "I figured that out."

"But I can't see you. I don't mean to sound dense but I can't even see your clothes." I leaned forward without knowing if I was leaning too far forward. "Does everything you touch become invisible?" I whispered.

"No. I'm just not wearing any clothes."

I sat back. "Are you serious?"

"Alice Trumbull. Naked." A hand took my hand and shook it.

"You mean to tell me you just walk around naked all the time?"

"No, I wouldn't drive a car naked. People need to see a driver in a car or they get very freaked out. That's why we meet at the Sheraton. They've got a nice big locker room in the gym. We can come in, get undressed, put everything in a locker. Some of the women even work out later. They've got a pool. We like to suggest you swim underwater though. If you do a stroke with a lot of splashing it can be upsetting to the guests." Alice Trumbull had a very nice voice, straightforward Midwestern, not sarcastic.

"Are there many of us here?"

"I'd say usually twelve to fifteen, though I suspect there are some others who just don't speak up."

"So how long have you been invisible?"

"Six months," she said.

I let out an audible gasp. I had never really considered that it could go on that long.

"And I'm not the senior member here, not by a long shot. Listen," she said, and I felt a comforting pat on my arm. "I know what this is like for you, all the questions, all the fears, how finding out there are other people like you makes it better and worse at the same time. It's scary as hell when you drop off the face of the earth and no one notices. I'm assuming no one has noticed."

"Not really," I said.

"Have you told your husband? I see you're still wearing a ring."

Sure enough, my ring was floating out there. "He doesn't know," I said.

"It took my husband four months to figure it out." Alice stood up. I could see the seat of her chair smooth out and feel the smallest shift in the air around me. "Come on, we'll get you a locker. It's time for the meeting to start."

"Why do I need a locker?" I asked. I stood up but didn't know which way to go until Alice took my sleeve and guided me along, the invisible leading the invisible.

"So you can store your clothes."

I stopped. "But I don't really want to take my clothes off."

"I know," she said, nudging me to move forward again, "but eventually you do. That's just part of it. And besides, if they see people sitting in a conference room with clothes on they'll ask us to leave. It's happened before."

I could feel a little invisible lump rising in the back of my throat. I was not what you'd call a naked person. I was the kid who changed her clothes in the toilet stall before gym class. Even now, if I'm walking from the bathroom to the closet after a shower, I put on a robe. To just stroll around my own house naked, even if no one was home and it was dark and the shades were down, no, it would never happen. So the idea of walking naked through the halls of the Sheraton—"Won't it be cold?"

Alice stopped. "Aren't you *ever* naked? None of us gets

hot or cold anymore. It's one of the perks of the invisible life—climate control."

"I guess I have noticed that," I said, feeling disappointed to have lost my best excuse.

"You need to hustle up," Alice said. "We're going to miss the reading of the last meeting's minutes and the introduction of new members, which would be you."

"Oh," I said. "Sure." I took off my jacket, my silk scarf. I sat down on the bench and unzipped my boots, pulled off my stockings. "Are you still here?"

"I can't *see* you," Alice said, sounding slightly exasperated. A locker door opened and my neatly stacked clothes floated up and landed inside. I took a deep breath and pulled off my underpants and bra. Then the door was closed. "Now hide your Kleenex inside your fist, like this. Nobody likes to see Kleenex floating down the hall."

How odd it was that someone would notice a Kleenex but not notice that the woman standing beside them had no head. We got on the elevator and took it up to the third floor. I crossed my arms over my breasts. The last time I'd gone braless I was twelve. "I'm not entirely comfortable with this," I said as a way of making conversation.

"It grows on you," she said. "Since I've been invisible I've come to see clothing as the Great Oppressor. Also, you wouldn't believe how much money you save. Clothes are really expensive."

We walked down the hallway and into the Magnolia Room, where a dozen chairs made a lazy circle beside a buffet table laid out with a coffee urn and a tray of Danish. Alice shook out the Kleenex in her hand and waved it like a flag over her head. "Friends, we have a newcomer today!"

Suddenly there was a flurry of Kleenex waving back and forth, a smattering of applause. One would think that as an invisible person myself I would look upon this non-sight, this empty room full of people, as the most comforting thing in the world. Sisterhood! Solidarity! But in fact I found the whole thing as creepy and disconcerting as I would have before when I walked Ohio in my full flesh. I thought of how Gilda must shiver a little bit every time I walked into her house and how bravely she had continued to love me when I wasn't there. I did my best to remember my manners. I unrolled my Kleenex and said hello.

"Come get your coffee and something to eat," a new voice said, very cheerful, sunny. "We don't eat during the meetings. It has to be before or after, otherwise someone from housekeeping walks in in the middle of a discussion and picks up all the plates. Do you want coffee?"

"Please," I said, trying to find my natural voice. "Black."

"Just like me," the voice said, and someone else laughed, though I didn't know if the speaker had meant she liked black coffee or was herself a woman of color. I actually found myself squinting, as if I might be able to see her if I just tried a little harder.

I turned around to take the cup and in doing so knocked someone's cherry Danish off their plate. "I'm so sorry," I said. If I had skin I would have been jumping out of it.

"You didn't see me," the woman said. Another voice, a

new one. "It's all right. That's what the Kleenex are for. Just try to keep it visible. 'Be Aware of Your Kleenex and Other People's Kleenex.' That's one of our first codes of conduct for the meetings."

"If you want to ask a question, raise your Kleenex and wait to be called on." I saw something glinting in front of me and realized the speaker was wearing contacts.

"I still think that's a little much," Alice said. I recognized her warm Midwestern vowels. "I don't think we need to dictate rules of social behavior."

"We rely on visual cues to know when we're supposed to talk. Now that the visual cues are gone we have to find reasonable substitutions."

All the voices were running together. Why couldn't we wear clothes? We could each chip in and pay for the cost of the conference room and wear our clothes. The hotel would take our money, our money wasn't invisible. If people were wearing clothes I could at least match a voice to a sweater. I felt like I was at my first social mixer at a school for the blind. I was just getting used to the fact that no one could see me—now I couldn't see anyone else either.

"We used to each carry white roses," someone said. "What a sentimental debacle that turned out to be."

"Why?" I asked. Certainly it was a lovelier gesture than the Kleenex.

"Well, for one thing, they were hard to come by, and if too many of us went to the same florist they were likely to get freaked out. Then there was the business of the thorns."

"And inevitably some little girl would come along and

snatch it right out of your hand, even on the street. Little girls are brazen thieves when it comes to unattended flowers."

"Once a girl walked into our meeting and picked up every single rose like she was some sort of bride or something and they had been put out just for her. She made herself a bouquet and then turned around and left."

"They never steal Kleenex."

The voices came at me from every direction and I couldn't begin to separate them out. It was like standing in the middle of a blizzard and trying to differentiate the snowflakes.

"Ladies," a voice said, raising itself above the others. "I think it's time for the meeting to come to order." But wait! I recognized that voice. It was the one who had been talking about the need for visual cues.

There was a shuffling among the group. Uneaten bits of Danish were dumped into a trash can or quickly eaten. The used plates were stacked, the used coffee cups arranged themselves into the same configuration they had been in to begin with. There were no smears of lipstick against the sides of the heavy china cups, no last few sips sitting coldly in the bottoms. Invisible women left things tidy, they way they had found them. It was as if we hadn't been there at all.

I went to sit down in a chair and sat instead in the wide naked lap of someone I did not see. My heart nearly stopped at that singular sensation of flesh against flesh. I bolted up. "My God," I said. "I'm so sorry."

"It happens," the woman said, her voice forgiving. "It takes some time to get this down. Just watch for the Kleenex."

"I now call the meeting of invisible women to order," another voice said.

"That's Jo Ellen. She's taking her presidency very seriously," Alice whispered in my ear. How did she know to sit beside me? How did she know that was my ear?

"I'm Jo Ellen, and I'm an invisible woman."

"Hi, Jo Ellen!" The group chimed.

"We have at least one new member today," Jo Ellen said. "She's with Alice. Alice, will you introduce your friend?"

"I'm sure we will be friends but the truth is I just found her in the lobby this morning. She was trying to ask the girl at the desk where the meeting was."

The group got a good laugh out of this. I was sitting naked among a group of strangers in the Sheraton and they were laughing at me. It was the stuff of grade school nightmares.

"I didn't even ask you your name," Alice said. "I'm losing all my social skills. You're going to have to do your own introduction."

"Do I stand up?"

"It's all the same to us," the woman on the other side of me said, the wearer of contacts. "Whatever makes you comfortable."

I stayed in my seat and gave my Kleenex a tentative flap. "My name is Clover Hobart, and I'm an invisible woman."

I heard a sharp, collective inhale go around the room.

"What?" I said.

"We don't use last names in the meetings."

"Why not? Alice told me her last name."

There was a long silence. Silence in a group of invisible women was not a comfortable thing. Had they left? Were they leaving? Should I leave?

"Why *don't* we use last names?" Alice asked.

"It's a little strange when you think about it," someone said on the other side of the circle. "It's not AA. I don't care who knows my last name."

"I'm Lila Robinson," a voice piped up. "Clover, I had Nick and Evie in my second-grade class at Brookside Elementary."

"Mrs. Robinson!" I said. The joy! I would have gone and hugged her had I known where she was. Oh, the children loved Mrs. Robinson! We would sing the song on the way to school every morning. *And here's to you, Mrs. Rob-in-son. Jeee-sus loves you more than you will know. Wo, wo, wo.* How old would Mrs. Robinson be now?

One by one the women went around the room giving their full names and waving their Kleenex, and after each one the rest of us said, "Hi, Alice Trumbull! Hi, Patty Sanchez!" Laura Worthington was there. She had been the weather girl on Channel Four a dozen years ago. She was willowy and blond with graceful hands that framed the cartoon images of smiling suns and angry clouds on the weather map. Everyone always said how much she looked like Vanna White.

"Well, now that we know who everybody is and no one has any anonymity anymore, do you suppose we can proceed with the meeting?" Jo Ellen asked.

A Kleenex went up on the other side of the circle. "Patty Sanchez. For the record, I have about as much anonymity as I can bear right now. And I love that Laura Worthington is in our group."

"For more than a year now," Laura said.

Together we made a small sound of wonder.

"Who'd like to tell their story today?" Jo Ellen said.

All the Kleenex stayed down for a while and then finally one gave a small flutter not too far from the seat of the chair. "Go ahead," Jo Ellen said.

"It's Lila Robinson again," Mrs. Robinson said.

"Hi, Lila."

"I have to say, having Clover here today has got me feeling a little emotional. Don't misunderstand me," she said quickly. "I'm glad you came. Sorry for you, of course, but glad to have somebody here I know from before. I had both of Clover's children in my class. They were very good children, lots of energy. Your Evie would have turned cartwheels all day long if I'd let her. Did she keep up with her gymnastics?"

"She's a cheerleader at Ohio State," I said. Something in me began to unclench the slightest bit.

"It makes me think about all the wonderful students I had," Mrs. Robinson said, the emotion coming up in her voice. "I was with the school system for almost thirty years but when I became invisible, bang, that was it. They were done with me. I think we could do with a few more invisible teachers, especially in the upper grades. Even if they couldn't use us in the classrooms teaching regular classes, we could still be hall monitors or test proctors. If you ask me there would be a lot less bullying if we had invisible teachers. But no, I wasn't normal. They thought I might upset the children. I told them I could come in naked, the children wouldn't even know I was there, but then they said I could be violating their civil liberties."

"Because of the nakedness or the fact they wouldn't know you were there?" someone snapped. Maybe it was Patty Sanchez. I wasn't positive.

"What about *your* civil liberties?" Laura Worthington said. Her voice I knew. *Be looking for sunshine around the middle of the week.*

"We aren't even covered by the Americans with Disabilities Act." There was a low tide of grumbling in the room.

"No one is interested in us," Mrs. Robinson said. "When I look back on my life, I was invisible for so many years before I became invisible. I never did stand up for myself. If you don't stand up before you become invisible, what chance do you have of making people pay attention to you when you aren't there?"

"Amen to that," a voice said.

We all had something to say now, all the Kleenex were up and people had started talking over one another. Jo Ellen raised her voice for order when all of a sudden the door to the Magnolia Room opened and a young Filipino woman pushing a cart came into the room. Instantly, we fell into a perfect silence, all of the Kleenex fluttering to the floor. Were we busted? I followed suit and dropped my tissue. The young woman stood in the door for a long time, her large, dark eyes sweeping the room from side to side. Finally she guided her cart over to the refreshment table. Like us, she made absolutely no sound. She was a tiny thing. The beige polyester uniform she wore was no doubt the smallest one they made and it was two sizes too big for her. She looked at the cups and the plates and, deciding they were actually dirty, loaded them onto her cart along with the coffee urn. She took a small bite off the edge of a cherry Danish and then picked up the tray. There she saw the twenty-dollar bill that someone in the group had left for her. After checking the door over her shoulder to make sure it wasn't a test, she plucked the money up and put it in the pocket of her uniform. She then went around the circle and picked up all the Kleenex off the carpet one by one before pushing her cart back out of the room. After a few minutes of waiting, someone finally got up and shut the door behind her.

"At least she didn't stack the chairs," someone said.

"Or vacuum."

Once we were alone again it felt as if some of our energy had left us. We were all thinking the same thing—that none of us was quite as invisible as that girl.

"Lila?" Jo Ellen said.

Mrs. Robinson sighed. "No, nothing else."

"But wait," I said, confused by what seemed to me to be a key point. "This is Clover again. There are people out there who know that we're invisible? I mean, it isn't a secret?"

"Absolutely not. The only time it's a secret is when we make it a secret out of shame or fear of rejection," a voice said, sounding like she was reading off part of the invisible women manifesto. "Plenty of people know we're there and they just continue to ignore us. They say we make them uncomfortable. They say they don't know how to deal with us. We don't fit in the system. Nobody talks about us."

We sat in silence with that one for a good long time. We were gone and no one missed us and none of us knew what to say.

"Next order of business," Jo Ellen said finally, trying to steer the meeting away from the topic, which had caused a good bit of sniffling in the circle. "Rosemary, do you have a medical report?"

Rosemary cleared her throat to pull herself together. "I've been calling Dexter-White every day. I actually got through to a senior chemist on Thursday, a total fluke. He agreed to meet me next week in the shampoo section of the Cheltenham Target at noon."

The group made a collective sound that was somewhere between hopefulness and pleasure, half *ooohhh* and half *aaahhh*. Only Rosemary was unimpressed by the news. "We'll see if he shows," she said.

"Dexter-White the pharmaceutical company?" I asked. "In Philadelphia?"

"One and the same," Rosemary said.

"What do they have to do with this?"

"Everything in the world," Alice said. "Assuming you're taking Premacore hormone replacement therapy, and Ostafoss calcium supplement, and Singsall antidepressant, all Dexter-White drugs."

"It's that exact combination for all of us," Rosemary said.

"Plus we've all tried Botox at least once, but we don't know if that has anything to do with it."

I had done this to myself? Someone had done this to me? Someone knew this was happening and still continued to do it to other women? "I'm assuming—"

"We've all stopped taking the pills," Jo Ellen said. "We're invisible, not stupid."

"It's a perfectly reasonable question," Mrs. Robinson said in my defense. "You don't need to be short."

"I've been looking at maps of Philadelphia," Rosemary said. "I think I've figured out how to get from the airport to the Target using public transportation."

"Couldn't you just take a taxi?" I asked. "Wear a coat and a hat. You can get a cab."

"True," Laura Worthington said. "But then you can't get on the plane."

"Anyway, I'd like someone to come with me, preferably someone with medical connections who knows how to ask questions."

The room fell quiet. No one seemed interested in flying to Philly. I had a husband and a brother who were doctors, and, even though it seemed like an impossibly long time ago, I had once been a reporter. "I'll do it," I said finally.

"Up and back in a day," Rosemary said, her voice sounding both happy and relieved. "No one's even going to notice you're missing."

five

When Gilda opened her door the next morning she looked down at Red. "When did you learn how to ring the bell?" she said.

"I picked him up so he could push it with his paw," I said.

Gilda put her hand to her heart and for an instant closed her eyes. "You scared me to death." She looked to the left and then to the right. "Where are you?"

"I'm right in front of you," I said. The air was laced with

decorative snow, tiny flakes being blown from side to side with no intention of sticking.

"Then why can't I see you?"

"Jeeze, Gilda, it's not like anything has changed. You know why you can't see me." I came in the house and Red followed behind, but Gilda stood stock-still in the middle of her entry hall, her hands spread out to either side.

"I don't understand what's going on," she said. "Are you in the house? Did you find some invisible clothes?"

"I'm not wearing clothes."

Gilda looked down at Red as if he were the one who was spreading rumors. "That isn't possible."

"It is, actually. I'm naked. I thought I would hate it but really, it feels kind of great." I touched her hand so she would know where I was and she yelped.

"It's freezing outside!"

"I know, but it doesn't bother me. It turns out I've got the invisible thermostat. All the women have it. We don't get cold and we don't get hot. It's sort of the reward for everything else."

"All what women?"

"That's what I came over to tell you. I went to a meeting of invisible women at the Sheraton yesterday." I passed by her and went into the kitchen to fill the kettle. "There were a dozen women there. Alice thinks there could be more who come and just don't say anything at first. They call them the wallflowers."

"Who's Alice?"

"She's one of the women I met. She was great. We went out for coffee after the meeting. She's an electrical engineer. She designs some kind of panel for computer chips. I didn't actually understand what she was talking about but it sounded really interesting. She works from home so becoming invisible wasn't as much of a hardship for her as it was for some of the other women. It turns out a lot of them get fired once they go through the change."

Gilda stopped and put her hands on her head. "I don't even know where to start," she said.

"I know. It was a lot for me to take in, too." I got down the box of tea bags. Gilda watched as they floated through the air.

"Wait a minute," she said, and went upstairs. She came back a minute later and handed me a pretty flannel bathrobe, a dark coral pink with a blue satin piping. I recognized it because it was the one I had given her for her birthday last year. "Please put this on."

I took it from her and held it in my hand. "Why? I'm not asking you to look at me naked."

"That's true, but frankly just the fact of it is making me uncomfortable." Then she whispered, "What if Miller comes downstairs?"

"It wouldn't make any difference. He can't see me."

"Well then put it on so I'll know where to look when I'm talking to you."

I put the bathrobe on, cinched the belt. True, it was petty and small-minded on her part, but since I had been liberated for exactly one day I knew I should cut her a break. "Better?"

"Thank you," she said. "So how did you even find out about this meeting?"

"I saw an ad in the *Herald*. I mean, what are the chances of that? All the years I've been looking over the want ads and this has been there and I've never seen it. It's so amazing when you think about it, like even their ads are invisible."

"How often do these meetings happen?"

"The new members' meetings are on Wednesdays. Those are the ones they advertise. But really, they have meetings all the time. And if you need a meeting and there isn't one you can go to the website and ask. Apparently people are really good about coming out."

"When did you see it?"

"See what?"

"The ad," Gilda said like she was running out of patience.

I stopped to think. It felt like it had been weeks ago. "Day before yesterday."

"And you didn't think it was worth mentioning?" Gilda was making herself busy with the cups but I could tell her feelings were hurt.

"I guess I just didn't want to talk about it. I didn't know what it was going to turn out to be like and I didn't want to get my hopes up."

"So what did you hope?"

I thought about it. I hadn't put it into words even to

myself. "That I wasn't going to be the only one. That I wasn't in this alone."

"Alone!" Gilda said. "How have you been alone in this? I've been with you every day."

"You have. You've been so great. But I wanted the chance to talk to other people this has happened to. They think it's all a reaction to drugs. Rosemary and I are going to fly to Philadelphia next week to meet with a chemist from Dexter-White."

"Rosemary. I guess she's another one of your little invisible friends."

I ignored that. "Some of the women in the group have flown all over the place. Alice flew to New York last week just to see the Gauguin exhibit and then came home. She waited in the taxi line at the airport until she heard somebody say they were going to the Upper East Side and then she climbed in with them. When they stopped at a light in front of the museum she just got out. If they think it's weird that the car door opens and closes by itself she doesn't care. The best part is she goes in the back door with the guards. She saw the whole show before they'd even opened. She has such ingenuity. I would never have come up with a plan like that."

"And how does she get on the plane? How do you use your ID when they can't see you?"

"You don't. You just go naked. You go around security and get on a plane, only you have to be the last one to sit down so nobody sits on you."

Gilda put her elbows on the kitchen counter and then put her head in her hands. "I feel like I'm going to be sick."

"Why?" I said, my patience starting to fray. "Because I'm figuring out how to function?"

"No! Because you're talking about breaching airport security to fly naked on a flight you haven't paid for. Doesn't that strike you as a little odd, Clover?"

"What strikes me as odd," I said, "is that my own best friend who is in perfect health can't be happy for her sick friend who's trying to lead a normal life."

"Hey, Mrs. Hobart," Miller said, walking into the kitchen. "Are you sick?"

"I'm fine, Miller. I'm just in a bad mood."

"I don't mean to pry," he said. His eyes were scanning the countertops, looking for food. "But I just heard you say you were sick, and you're wearing my mom's bathrobe."

"Okay," I said. "I don't feel great. But don't worry. It isn't contagious."

"I thought you were driving your brother to school," Gilda said.

Miller picked up the car keys and jingled them. "I just came in for these. I hope you feel better, Mrs. Hobart."

"Thanks, Miller."

Once the boys were gone I looked at Gilda and she looked at her bathrobe. "I'm sorry," she said.

"No," I said. "It's me. You really have been great."

"This is an adjustment, that's all. We always did everything together."

"I know," I said. "But trust me, this isn't something you want to do."

After Gilda and I had reached a shaky détente I headed back across the street, where, from a distance, I saw my mother-in-law sitting on my front porch. I was in a bit of a quandary because I'd given the bathrobe back. I'd left the front door open but the back door was locked so I couldn't sneak around and get dressed. I wasn't even sure that getting dressed would be enough to fool Irene. To make matters worse, Red was now barking and hopping and straining against his leash to get to her. Red, who loved everyone, loved my mother-in-law above all others.

"Hello, Redster," she said, crouching down into a perfect yogic squat to rub his ears. "How's my good boy?" For a minute I could see her puzzle over the taut leash, then she unclipped it. It was a retractable leash, and it retracted at the speed of light, giving my shins a sharp smack before whipping back into the casing. I gave out an involuntary yip.

"Clover?"

"Hi, Irene."

She stood up and put her hand over her eyes to block the sun. "You're invisible?"

That was Irene, calling it like she saw it. "I am. I should have told you."

She came down the stairs in her dark purple yoga pants

and fuzzy gray sweater, her silver hair cropped short and shimmering in the morning light. At seventy-six she put every woman I knew to shame. She walked right over and took me into her arms. "Oh, darling, I'm so sorry."

For a second I wondered how she had found me so easily but then I remembered I was still holding the leash. Irene wouldn't care if I was naked. Irene would think naked was a grand idea. "You don't seem surprised," I said.

"Well, I *am* surprised. I didn't know what was going on, only that it was something. When you didn't come to class and you didn't call me back I started to worry. Then when Arthur called and said you were depressed—"

"He's got to stop that."

She shook her head. "He wants you to be fine but he wants someone else to take care of it for him, me or Evie or Gilda, one of the women in your life. He puts out these messages hoping one of us will fix things for him. And look, here I am! I'm not asking you to have too much compassion for Arthur but it's got to be confusing for him, having his wife just vanish. It's always harder for doctors. They think they should be able to fix everything. Arthur's father used to get so impatient with me whenever I was sick and I wouldn't get better right away."

We went into the house. Red was still jumping all over Irene and I gave him a chew stick to take his mind off her for a minute. "Arthur doesn't know I'm invisible," I said.

"What are you talking about?"

"Neither does Nick for that matter. They know something is different but they just can't quite put their finger on it."

Irene sat down slowly at the kitchen table. "Tell me you're joking."

"I should have told them, but I didn't. The more time goes by the more I have this crazy notion that they should be able to figure it out for themselves."

"But you're right!" Irene said, and slapped the table in front of her with both hands. "They have to figure it out."

"Arthur's always so busy. It seems like every year his practice doubles. Everybody's always pulling on him, wanting something. And poor Nick can't find a job. He's really trying. He's so distracted right now I don't think he'd notice if I had a raccoon growing on the side of my head." I thought about this for a minute. "No, I'm pretty sure he wouldn't notice that."

"Stop making excuses for them. You're invisible. It isn't too much to ask that they might notice. They have eyes! They can see that the toilet paper roll needs changing and the wastebasket is full and that there is no more orange juice and we drink orange juice and orange juice is sold in grocery stores. They've trained themselves not to notice things because the less they notice the more we'll just take care of it for them. They say, you should have told me you wanted my help when we had twelve people coming over for dinner! You should have told me not to sit in front of the computer looking at football scores while you're running around doing everything by yourself. If you needed my help why didn't you ask for it? I didn't know you needed help. It's madness. I wanted to raise my son to be better than this, but I was so young when he was born, and I was so in love with him, I think I must have done too much for him. I wanted to raise him to be helpful and thoughtful and attentive and for a while he was, but somewhere along the line, I don't know, he jumped the rails."

"It was me," I said, and I knew it was true. "It was losing my job and being home more. It made everything so much easier. I paid the bills and made the meals and changed the lightbulbs and shoveled the snow and wrote the thank-you notes and planned the vacations and raised the children." I had to cut myself off. I realized I could go on like this for the rest of the day without taking a breath.

"This is a disaster," Irene said. "I'm terribly sorry you're invisible but the idea that you've had to go through all of this by yourself—"

"Gilda's been great," I said. "And Red." Red was sitting in my lap. Now that I had stopped wearing clothes he appeared to be levitating above the chair. "He's the only one who can still see me."

"He doesn't see you," Irene said. "He smells you. Dogs respond first to what they smell."

"Oh," I said, feeling slightly disappointed, then I remembered where I was going with this. "I've joined an invisible women's support group. I found an ad in the paper."

"That ad has been running for years. I had a student who

was invisible once, Jane Sidwell. *She* kept coming to class," Irene said pointedly.

"What happened to her?" I asked. I hadn't been brave enough to ask the women in the group. Have any of us ever shown up again? What becomes of us in the long term?

"Her family moved to New York. She also wanted to be closer to Dexter-White. Do you know about Dexter-White?"

"I do," I said. "Though I guess I was the last one to find out."

"I should have told you. I just never knew you were taking . . ." Irene shook her head as if shaking the thought away. "It doesn't matter. Jane went to Philadelphia several times a week and went through their offices, read their e-mails, made copies of files. Apparently she was all over that place."

"But don't they have a huge security system?"

Irene shrugged. "What's security to an invisible woman? It wasn't as if she had to break into the building after hours. She'd sit right on the desk of the CEO. She'd listen to his letters as he was dictating them. Sometimes she would even mess around with him a little, blow in his ear, move the furniture, that sort of thing. She's become quite the poltergeist."

"But is she still invisible?"

Irene nodded. "The last I heard, yes, but that was several months ago. Maybe her situation has improved by now. I'll give you her e-mail address. In the meantime, I suggest you take a page from Jane's book. Seize the day. Go out there and do the things you've always wanted to do. Don't sit around hoping that someone's going to notice that you're missing. Invisibility can be an impediment or a power depending on what you decide to do with it."

"I stopped a man from yelling at a woman in a parking lot a few days ago. I didn't know what was going on exactly but I got in between them."

"There you go!" Irene said, taking my hand. "You're practically a superhero already."

That night, when Arthur and I were lying in bed in the dark, I asked him, "If you could have any superhero power, which one would you want?"

"Flight," he said without a moment's reflection. "Wouldn't everyone want to be able to fly?"

"I don't know," I said, trying to work toward my intended topic of conversation indirectly. "Maybe somebody would want to have x-ray vision or superhuman strength."

"It would be nice to have a germ shield," he said. "That would probably improve the quality of my life more than anything else. There could be an entirely new comic book line—Germ Man. He never has to wash his hands or wear gloves. Kids can sneeze all over him and he never catches anything. The tag line would be 'Germs bounce off like bullets.' What do you think?"

"He wouldn't just repel germs," I said into the dark, a sliver of silvered moon shining through the window. "He would explode them. He emits some kind of high-pitched frequency that only germs can hear, because he's discovered that germs *can* actually hear, so that everyone he comes in contact with who has any sort of an infection would be instantly healed."

Arthur scooted toward me in the bed, spooned me into his arms. "You're a genius, do you know that? I was only thinking of the self-preservation aspect but you took Germ Man to the next level. You made him a humanitarian. That's what superheros have to be after all. You can't just be a self-preservationist superhero."

"Germ Man could walk through cholera epidemics in Haiti and heal the sick just by going past them. He could go to AIDS clinics in Africa and everyone would hop off their cots and follow him out into the streets."

"And when he's not saving the sick, he's locked in mortal combat with brilliant mad scientists who are trying to hold the world hostage with germ warfare." Arthur ran his tongue along the rim of my ear. "I'm finding this very sexy," he said.

"You could be Germ Man," I said. "And I could be your faithful sidekick, Clover Hobart, who has been injected by an evil scientist with such a virulent germ that the only way you can overpower it is by making love to her."

In truth, invisibility had put quite a kick in our sex life. Passion was the one thing that was keeping me connected to Arthur. It allowed me to forgive him for everything he was missing. It was also one of the few times I felt completely there, like nothing in my body had changed.

"My poor, germ-laden Clover Hobart," he whispered in my ear, pulling his hand up my thigh.

It was wonderful, don't get me wrong. I loved it. But still, I had been hoping he would have said at some point, "So Clover, what superhero power would you most like to have?" That could have been part of the game as well.

six

The next day I called Lila Robinson, who I was trying not to call Mrs. Robinson in my mind. She wasn't that much older than I was. I got her number off our local invisible women's website, www.invisibleme.com. Turns out it was there all along, it's just about 200,000 hits down on Google. When she answered at the end of the first ring I suspected that she might be spending too much time at home.

"I've been thinking a lot about what you said in the meeting," I told her.

"There is an awful lot of time to think these days," she said. Her voice sounded tired.

"What I think," I said, "is if you still want to be at the school, then what's to keep you from going there? I mean, you aren't going to get a paycheck, but would you want to be there even if you weren't getting paid?" I was trying to utilize Irene's advice, become proactive.

"They don't want me," she said. "They made it very clear."

"Okay, say for now we forget about what they want. Why can't we do good where we see good needs doing? Why do we have to sit home waiting for permission to do what's right? We have a superpower. We're the rarest creatures in the world. Maybe it's not our first choice but here we are. Shouldn't we make something out of it?"

"Clover, what are you talking about?"

Maybe we didn't know each other that well. Maybe we knew each other better than any two more-or-less strangers ever would. "I'm talking about this: if you found out that tomorrow you were going to become permanently and irrevocably visible again, what would you regret not doing that you didn't do while you had the chance?"

The other end of the line stayed quiet. Lila was sketching it out in her head. "I'd want to ride the school bus and stop the bullies," she said finally. "I'd want to go to the school and keep the bad kids from doing bad things they didn't really want to do. I'd want to figure out a way to give the loser kids a boost and settle down the classrooms so the teachers can teach. And then I'd want to go to Tiffany's and try on enormous diamond rings."

This last one I wasn't expecting. "Seriously?"

"You asked."

"So the bus tomorrow?"

"I think you're crazy," she said, but I could already hear the yes in her voice. I knew I'd hardly have to tap her to push her over the edge.

"Listen, pretty soon I'm going to have to fly to Philadelphia to break into the offices of a pharmaceutical company and find out what they know about the fact that they've poisoned us. I've got to get outside my comfort zone immediately. I think a high school and some diamonds would be just the thing."

"I'll be on the bus in the morning," she said. "Be sure to bring a Kleenex."

In the morning it was raining. Rosemary had called the night before to tell me the Dexter-White guy had postponed our meeting. High school now felt like small potatoes. Benny Kempton was waiting on the corner for the bus. Benny almost never took the bus—Steve or Gilda or Miller drove him to school. Maybe this morning everyone was busy. I went and stood behind him, wishing that Benny was the sort of kid who believed in umbrellas, but I guess no high school boy believed in umbrellas. He wore the rubberized hood of his rubberized raincoat pulled up while the water sluiced off my invisible head and down onto my invisible, naked body. I may as well have been standing in the shower.

Benny sniffed the air. "Mrs. Hobart?" he said, and turned around to look behind him.

It was true, I'd been wearing a little more perfume lately. I thought it helped people locate me, even though I wasn't so interested in being located by Benny. I kept my mouth shut. In the distance I could see the school bus wobbling up the road. The closer it came to us the more Benny started to shift his weight from side to side, like maybe he was thinking about breaking into a sprint in the opposite direction. Why was Benny on the bus this morning? Why did Benny never take the bus?

As soon as the doors swung open, I knew. As he climbed up the stairs the bus erupted into a chorus of heckles and catcalls. "It's the bone man!" the boys called out. "It's the boner!" The girls turned away, laughing like jackals. It was an easy bit of cruelty, as Benny, so thin and suddenly tall, looked like a model in an anatomy textbook. I could see the wings of his shoulders curve down on themselves as he slumped ahead, dripping wet. His soaking lunch bag tore in half beneath the weight of its plastic-wrapped tuna sandwich. The apple he'd brought rolled under the seats, never to be seen again. "His mommy makes him lunch!" the boys crowed. As if their mommies didn't do the same. I had one foot on the stairs when the bus doors tried to snap closed, very nearly snapping me in half.

"Come on," the driver said, yanking repeatedly on the handle of the door as if he were trying to manually detach my foot from my leg.

"Will you ease up on that thing?" I said. Grabbing on to the handrail, I dropped my Kleenex. It flew out the door and settled into a puddle on the pavement.

The driver squinted and opened the door again. "Some-body else getting on?" he said. A few of the smaller kids, the ones who sat in the very front of the bus and said their prayers, leaned forward to look but saw nothing. The driver shifted into drive. I leaned over, picked up Benny's sand-wich, and stuck it in the zippered compartment of his backpack.

It may seem counterintuitive, but it is not necessarily the goal of invisible people to go unnoticed. In fact, I saw a whole world of beauty and injustice I had never dared to no-tice before and I feel it is my right to act on it. Kids sprawled across their seats, pushing their wet coats and backpacks over any empty spaces, denying Benny the right to sit down. The bus driver hit the brakes and we all lurched forward. I thumped into a chubby boy and knocked his breakfast Pop-Tart out of his hand. "Hey!" he said, turning to look for a fight.

"Sorry," I said. Mine was a grown-up's voice, a mother's voice, and so the kid turned back with a distinctly rattled expression.

"Everybody's got to be sitting down," the driver said without inflection. "Do I need to tell you this every morn-ing? We don't go forward until everyone takes a seat. That's the rule of the bus."

I chose a pretty girl with chestnut hair and a raspberry-colored sweater who was wearing less makeup than your average Las Vegas showgirl. I picked up her books, her bag, and her enormously puffy coat and, rolling them together, I placed them on her lap. Suddenly a seat became available and Benny, bless his heart, thought that he had actually caught a break, that this was his invitation. He sat down beside her, careful to keep his soaking coat away from her thigh, though in truth everything was wet. "Thanks," he mumbled very quietly.

A look of panic and disgust crossed her pretty face as she stuffed her iPod buds into her ears and pressed herself against the window.

"Jessica's got the boner!" a boy across the aisle shouted.

"Boner! Boner! Boner!" the chorus answered.

I pinched that first boy's earlobe hard between my thumb and forefinger. I would eventually get to all of them. "I know your mother," I whispered, though this was in fact a lie. I licked my lips before letting them touch his ear. "Start behaving like she's going to hear about all of this, because she will."

The boy sprang to his feet. Using his earlobe as a lever I sat him down again. "Decency," I said softly. "That's your word for today. I'm right here watching you."

It's true, I wished I had some clothes on. Being naked in the Sheraton among your peers was one thing, being naked among raging children was quite another. I did not enjoy the unpleasant sensation of vulnerability but these are the moments that build character. I leaned across Benny and tugged one of the tiny speakers from Jessica's ear. "You're a nice girl," I said. "Act like it."

She looked at Benny but he was staring at his own knee, his entire body pivoting away from her. She looked up, her eyes locked so directly onto mine that it startled me. "I'm your conscience," I said, a terribly corny line. "I'm strongly suggesting that you do the right thing." Benny was once again sniffing the air.

"Do you smell something?" he said to the girl very quietly. "Like something nice?"

She sniffed. She was practically sniffing my neck. "It's perfume," she said. She sniffed again. "It's Rive Gauche. It's the perfume my mom wears." She gave a little shudder along with her recognition. I could hardly believe my good luck. "It's like my mom is on the bus," she whispered to Benny.

"Jessica and Ben are kissing!" shouted three girls who were three rows behind them. They then broke out in an ecstatic pantomime of kissing one another that no doubt the boys would all be remembering later on in bed tonight.

Jessica turned in her seat and raised her voice to high. "Would you *shut* the fuck up now?" The girls, startled, surprised even themselves by doing what they were told. Jessica sat back down, keeping her eyes straight ahead. "My mom's been telling me to be nicer," she said to the seat back in front of her.

"I think you're doing a great job," Benny said.

Every few minutes the bus stopped and another one or two children would creep on looking like they were boarding a transport helicopter for the deserts of Afghanistan. Sensing fresh prey, the tougher kids began to ridicule and torment the newcomers, and so left Benny and Jessica alone in the wake of their carnage. Seats were denied the newcomers and so I found them seats. I thumped the heads of horrible girls, pinched the collarbones of terrible boys, not hard enough to hurt them but enough to get their attention so that I could whisper words of moral betterment in their ears. It was like performing some sort of social triage. I would stanch the flow of cruelty from one mouth only to see it burble forward in another. When finally we pulled up in front of the school I was utterly spent. I collapsed onto the long bench seat in the back and found it to be sticky and wet and unpleasantly warm. That was when I heard Lila's voice. I had forgotten all about her.

"Are you still on the bus?" she said.

"Back row," I said.

She came and sat beside me. "I lost my Kleenex," she said.

"The Kleenex never stood a chance." I put my head in my hands. "That was the most harrowing thing I've ever done in my life."

"They should raise the bus driver's pay by about two hundred thousand dollars a year."

"I never want to get on a school bus again, and at the same time I don't want to think of those poor children riding around without someone invisible."

"It's only eight a.m." Lila said. "We haven't even started."

Had I ever spent the day in our neighborhood public high school as an invisible woman while my children were still enrolled there, I no doubt would have insisted on home schooling. Lila and I had our work cut out for us: patrolling the stairwells, gently pressing unruly students back in their chairs during classes, removing countless iPod buds from countless ears so that we could whisper in the importance of respectful attention. After stopping at least a dozen students from cheating on an Algebra II exam while the teacher sat at her desk reading a back issue of *People* magazine, I broke up a small extortion ring in the bathroom, three bigger boys who were promising to pierce the ear of a much smaller boy if he didn't show up with a significant cut of his allowance. Lila and I had agreed to meet up again at a back left-hand corner table in the cafeteria at 12:30. There was barely enough time to wrestle the poor child away from his predators and get to lunch.

"I have never worked this hard," I said, dropping down in my chair. "Not once. Not ever." I'd brought a few squares of toilet paper along with me. As best as I could tell there wasn't a single Kleenex in the entire institution. Lila had snagged a paper napkin to be her marker.

"But it's exhilarating, isn't it? Don't you feel exhilarated?" Lila's voice was bright and full of wonder. She sounded like the second-grade teacher I knew when my children were small.

"Seriously? I feel like I've been hit by a truck."

"You were completely right about our just going ahead and coming over here. This is what we need to be doing! Kids don't want to be bad, they just have no idea how to stop themselves. They're so wrapped up in their image they can't make the right choices. That's why we're so good at helping them. We don't have any image. They can't feel threatened by us."

"I hope they feel a little threatened," I said. I had never threatened so many people in my life as I had this morning. I saw an unfortunate girl standing stock-still in the middle of the cafeteria holding her tray, as frozen as all the deer in all the collective headlights of humanity. "Just a minute," I sighed to Lila. I walked over to the lost child, who was burdened with both bad skin and bad hair and was trying to make up for all of that with a very tough-looking pair of combat boots. With a single finger on her shoulder, I gently steered her to a table of girls who I noticed had behaved decently for the entire day. I pulled out a chair and dropped her into it. "Hi!" I said brightly. The girls all looked around, trying to figure out where the voice had come from, but as they lacked the powers of complex reasoning there was nothing they could do but accept it.

"Well done," Lila said upon my return. "You should have been a teacher."

"Or the cafeteria lady. Either way, I'm not cut out for this."

"Of course you are! You've been saving lives all day. You'll get used to the mayhem. After a while you start to thrive on it."

"I won't get used to it," I said. "This was a one-shot deal for me."

Lila leaned forward and managed to find my hand. "Listen, you have to come back. They need you. I need you."

"You don't need me. You're in your element. You just needed somebody to get you back in the door. In a couple of weeks you'll have this place so shipshape you'll be able to make a case for getting your job back. As far as I'm concerned, I'll admit it, it's been good for me. I'm starting to think we need invisible women everywhere, not just for protection but to give people a nudge to be their better selves. That said, high school is not my environment. I think I'd be better off on Wall Street gently guiding the bankers and the hedge fund managers toward decency."

That was when the bell rang and we both looked sadly up at the clock. "Meet me at the bus at three," Lila said. I watched her chair push back from the table as she set out to make the school a safer place for education.

I hung in there for a long time but I'll admit I didn't make it all the way through to the end. I lost my way in a study hall that would have tried the patience of Gandhi. I found myself randomly smacking kids on the back of the head as they pushed *The Great Gatsby* aside to text and talk and pummel one another with spitballs. I harassed them and spooked them and reasoned with them as if I were their dead grandmother looking down on them from heaven with disappointment, but nothing worked for more than three minutes. Every three minutes they pushed some internal reset button and their world began anew. The ones I had steered toward their better selves relapsed almost instantly, leaving me to start it all again. Exhausted and defeated, I finally left them to their deviant ways and went to sit by myself in the bleachers that surrounded the baseball diamond. By myself! Have there ever been two more beautiful words?

That was when I heard Benny laughing.

I had listened to Benny Kempton laugh since he was three years old and that particular sputtering giggle, the one he used when he really got going, was dear to my heart. I finally found him by looking down between the slats of the bleachers. There he was, underneath and in a corner, laughing with Jessica. Jessica from the bus! Way to go, Benny! But then the breeze shifted directions and I caught a whiff of their merriment. Benny and Jessica were smoking a joint during last period.

I would say at that moment I was the unhappiest invisible woman in the world. I didn't want to know what Benny was doing. I didn't want to see it or smell it. I wanted to know nothing other than he had, at least for the afternoon, gotten the girl. I didn't want to bust their happiness, nor did I want this good boy to get busted by someone else who might deal with him harshly, nor did I especially want him to get away with it because Benny could so easily be a pothead and that was nothing but misery. I owed it to Benny and the girl to break it up. I owed it to Gilda. I owed it to Arthur, who had gone to the trouble of removing a grape from this child's windpipe when he was three years old. I hauled myself up and walked softly down the bleachers. Poor lambs, they never saw me coming.

I went and sat beside them in the grass. Jessica was laughing now, the wind-chime laugh of a beautiful girl. I could see the wonderment on Benny's face, the stark gratitude for this perfect moment I was about to ruin. He handed Jessica the joint. She laughed once more and inhaled.

"Look, kids," I began.

Jessica's head shot up. She ground the joint into the grass and sat on it. Benny raised up on his knees, his torso craning in every direction.

"It's too late," I said. "I've already seen it."

"It's the Rive Gauche again!" Jessica said, sniffing the air like a beagle. "It's my mother. I smell her." She looked around and, seeing nothing, closed her eyes tight. "What are you doing to me?"

I sniffed my own wrist. I found it hard to believe any trace of perfume had survived the day but the girl was right, it lingered there.

"It's not your mother," Benny said, his nose tracing the air. "It's the lady from the bus this morning."

"You heard a lady on the bus, too?"

"She sounds exactly like our neighbor," Benny said.

"I'm not your mother or your neighbor," I said, winging it as I went along. "The brain makes these voices into people you know so that Jessica hears me as one person and Benny hears me as another."

"How do you know our names?" the girl wailed. I thought she was going a little over the top.

"Because I'm you, and you know your own name. It isn't

complicated. This is what happens to people who smoke pot. Maybe some people can do it but the two of you can't. You're not chemically wired for it. It's going to wreck you. You're going to hear me badgering you every time you try. You're going to get caught, you're going to get suspended, your parents are going to find out, you won't get into college, you'll wind up working at Dunkin' Donuts."

Maybe I was laying it on a little thick but heavens, it was nicer than anything the principal would say were they dragged into his office. Jessica was crying openly now, Benny pushing the sleeve of his sweatshirt against his eyes. I gave them a minute to sit with this bitter picture of their future.

"Or," I said, as if presenting an equally plausible scenario, "you can skip all of that, say that was your last joint, and go on to have happy, successful lives."

"How are you so sure pot doesn't agree with us?" Benny said with a trace of skepticism.

"You're hearing voices. You're both hearing the same voices. Believe me, once you get to this phase there's no going back."

"It's never happened to me before," Benny said.

"I'll be sure to tell your mother that," I said.

Jessica started scrambling to gather up her books and get the hell out of there. I put my hand on her wrist. "Look, now you've got something to bond over. You can be the kids who don't smoke pot together. There are a lot of other ways to have fun. Take the money you save and go to the movies. Benny, ask Jessica to go to the movies."

He looked at her for a minute, cocking his head as if wondering if she was hearing the same thing. "Do you want to go to the movies on Saturday?"

Jessica waited to see if I would answer for her but when I didn't she gave a very small nod. "Okay."

I didn't announce my exit. I thought it was better to let them keep on thinking I was there for a while. Pot was good for paranoia. I walked away marveling at the powers of the unseen. Had I given them the exact same talk while they were looking at me they probably would have blown the smoke in my face. But as an invisible person I had real gravitas. I walked across the playing field feeling triumphant, then went and took my place behind the bus driver, where I found Lila, her paper napkin reduced to a tiny shred.

"When he gets to Jefferson we'll get off and walk over to the mall," I said, my voice quiet enough to stay hidden beneath the cacophony of teenagers recently released from school. Whereas in the morning they had possessed a savage cruelty, in the afternoon they were singing along with their iPods, bouncing up and down in their seats, hanging out the windows, drawing pictures in magic marker on one another's thighs. They had all been released from prison and now they were planning to party together.

"It's okay," Lila said. "I was just being silly. I know you're tired."

"I don't think I ever wanted to go to Tiffany's and try on diamonds before," I said. "But I'd never spent an entire day in a high school, that is, since I was last in high school myself. They didn't have a Tiffany's in the mall back then."

And so we hopped off the bus like a couple of errant schoolgirls, opening the door for ourselves while the poor, beleaguered driver raged at what he could not see or understand. I felt like screaming with joy just to be away from those kids. "How do you do it?" I said to Lila. "I mean without killing them or killing yourself. How, how, how?"

"Here, take my hand," Lila said. "I don't want to lose you." There we were, the invisible, naked women holding hands. "When I started teaching I was with the little kids and I loved them. I loved your kids. But after a while I wanted to do something more challenging. I wanted to read books that didn't have ponies or trains on the cover. I went back and got certified for high school and at first it was great because my high school students had all been my second-graders once and we all loved one another. Those kids really tried for me. They minded me the same way they had when they were little. It was some kind of Pavlovian thing, I guess. The sound of my voice made them sit up straight and quiet down. For a few years it was all really great, but then the kids who were coming in weren't kids I'd taught before, and I had to learn how to control them on my own. In the end it really isn't so different from teaching second grade. You just have to always be bigger than they are. Even when you're not bigger physically."

"Do you have kids of your own?" I asked. I really knew nothing about Lila Robinson, other than that I used to sing her name in the car with my children.

"Three," she said. "All grown up. I'm a grandmother now. A very young grandmother, but still. If you could see me you would swear it wasn't possible."

We both laughed. We walked in through Macy's and I told Lila I wanted to go to the perfume counter. "I need to freshen up," I said. I found a bottle of Rive Gauche and she picked up the Chanel No. 5. We gave ourselves a healthy spritz.

"Now I'll know how to find you," she said.

On the way to the mall we walked through the shoe department. I would very much have liked to be wearing shoes. My feet were unaccustomed to so much unsupported work. I passed a table full of high heels and thought how much they looked like fancy sleds with impossibly long nails sticking out the bottom. They were fantastically nonsensical. No one in the world, no one, would wear high heels if there was nobody who could see you do it.

It was nowhere near Thanksgiving and already the mall was tricked out for Christmas, green boughs and white lights and flashing tinsel decking the endlessly long halls. "Do you still have to meet everyone's holiday expectations if you're invisible?" Lila asked.

"No, once you're invisible you realize that it wasn't about other people's expectations in the first place. It was always about your anticipation of other people's expectations. If they don't miss me they certainly aren't going to miss a Christmas tree."

"Your husband hasn't noticed yet?" she asked.

I shook my head, that pointless gesture. "Nope."

"He will," she said, and squeezed my hand.

"Does Mr. Robinson know you're gone?"

"Mr. Robinson is blind," she said. "So I had to tell him. He said it was all the same to him. I never thought of blindness as a good thing until I started going to those meetings and listening to everyone else's story. Larry's taught me a lot about how to deal with a disability."

"Well," I said. "That's a healthy dose of perspective."

"Perspective is what it's all about," Lila said as we walked in to see the diamonds.

Tiffany's was crowded with young couples holding hands and teenaged girls longing for charm bracelets and matrons looking at china and nervous men looking at rings. Everything in the store sparkled and flashed, but discreetly. It didn't really dazzle until you were right up against the cases. "I've never done this," I said. We passed a necklace that made me stop, clusters of diamond flowers that looked as though they should have been draped around Audrey Hepburn's neck.

"Never been in here? Oh, I've been in here, but I've never had the nerve to try anything on. The gentlemen in the suits are very polite, always asking what they can show me. I guess they operate on the assumption that you never know who's rich. It makes me feel like a terrible fraud."

We stepped behind the counter, away from the crowd, and even that felt illegal. Still, the view was a lot easier to take in from the other side.

"I don't want a big diamond," she said. "I promise you, I'm way beyond that."

"That doesn't mean you shouldn't try one on," I said.

We went and stood next to one of the gentlemen, who had opened a case to show a modest ring to a boy not much older than Nick. Perish the thought. I reached in and picked up a little number the size of a robin's egg. It had a considerable heft, and I moved it slowly so that no one would see it flying off. It was such a strobe light, that ring, it was hard not to notice. "Something like this?" I said.

It was fun, crazy fun, and all the raucous hormones of high school fell away as we engaged in what felt like a very grown-up activity. "Oh my," Lila said. "You've got a good eye for this."

A good eye for diamonds, who knew! She put her hand down on the counter and slid the ring on so that if anyone was looking for it they would see that the ring was right there. We stared at it. It twinkled. We blinked.

"Oh," Lila said.

"Hmm," I said.

"Sort of needs a hand," she said.

"A hand is certainly what's missing."

"Somehow I hadn't thought about that part." She turned her nonexistent hand from side to side.

"Maybe a different ring?" I suggested. "A ruby?"

"No," she said, "I really think the problem would still be the same."

"Do you want to try one of the big necklaces?"

She took the ring off and nestled it back into its velvet slot. "Then I think I'd need to have a neck."

"So I guess that means the earrings are out too." We laughed a little now that we could see the folly of our desires.

The gentleman straightened up, sniffed the air. "Can I help you ladies?" he asked, looking to his right and his left, polite even to the invisible.

"Just looking," Lila said, and we stepped back to the public's side of the showcase and then went back into the mall. "That was really very liberating," she said once we were outside. "I wouldn't have guessed that."

"Me neither," I said. We were doubly lucky that day. Not only did we discover that we didn't want diamonds, as soon as we stepped up to the curb we found a bus to take us near enough to home.

By the time I got home I was exhausted. I sat in a hot bath and rubbed my aching feet. The bathtub was still a bit unnerving: the displacement of clear water by a clear person made a disconcerting visual for a person who otherwise had no visuals. I dried off and put on some more perfume, a sweat suit, and some big, plushy slippers and went downstairs to make dinner. Arthur called at 6:30 to say he was finished, he was walking out the door, but I knew better than to fall for that. He came in an hour later.

"Germ Man's invisible shield has failed him," he said, dropping his coat over the back of the couch. "I must have seen twenty kids with the flu today and every single one of them wanted to kiss me."

"Come sit down," I said. "Do you want a glass of wine?"

"What I'd love is a hot rum toddy with some honey and lemon." He worked his tie from side to side and unbuttoned his collar. "I don't mean to complain," he said.

"No, please," I said. "Do."

"I just wish you could spend one day in the office with me, just see what it's like start to finish. I don't think you'd even believe it. Crying children, crying parents, fifty phone messages to return, dictation, insurance companies to fight with, nurses who want to come in and tell me all their personal problems, a baby with a very suspicious rash and now I'm worrying about her. I'm nowhere close to retirement but when I think about doing this for another ten or fifteen years it just doesn't seem possible."

I felt for him, I really did. I knew how hard he worked. I would have loved for him to say "Tell me what happened to you today. Anything exciting?" but the most exciting thing that ever happened to me anymore was getting a galley of a decent book to review. It probably no longer occurred to him to ask.

Which is all by way of saying, I had never meant to have a secret life, but now I did.

seven

*A*s for the issue of clothing versus nakedness, I found that neither one was the perfect answer for every occasion. As a result, I seemed to run a straight fifty/fifty split. There were times that clothes just felt appropriate—Irene's yoga class, for example, where I simply could not imagine getting into downward dog in a roomful of people regardless of whether or not they could see me. For one thing, I appreciated her adjustments and comments on my form, which she could manage easily as long as I had on a pair of sweatpants and a long-sleeved T-shirt.

"Sit bones reaching up," she said, her voice melodic, soothing. "Chest toward the floor."

I was glad to be back under her instruction. I needed to stretch. I needed to be reminded to breathe. Out of sight, out of mind, as the old adage goes. I had been slack when it came to looking after that which I could not see. As for the other women in the class, they noticed nothing unusual about me. Irene preached the doctrine of focus turned inward. "Yoga is not a competitive sport," she said as she walked between our mats. "Stop looking around."

I stayed in shavasana until everyone else had left, lying on my mat like the invisible dead. "Arthur is always saying he wishes I could watch one of his days start to finish," I told his mother, my eyes still closed. "He was talking about it again last night and I thought, why not? No time like the present."

"Maybe he's feeling unseen," she said. "It's possible that that's the lesson in all of this, not who sees you but who you can learn to see."

Irene was sitting in lotus position on the floor beside me wearing white pants and a white top. "My mother-in-law, my guru," I said.

She laughed. "I'm not telling you what to do, but it does seem like you have a real opportunity in front of you. I know this is a hardship, but I have to say there are certain elements of your life I envy. You have a new perspective on everything. You're both learning about yourself and learning to break away from yourself, at least in the more trivial aspects."

I thought about the diamonds, the high-heeled shoes. "You have a point."

"Go find out what Arthur's day is like," she said. "And then tell me. I'd be curious to know."

"Could you drop me off at his office?" I asked. Irene had very nicely picked me up at the house this morning, a teacher's best bet for ensuring her student would come to class.

"But then how will you get home?"

"I'll catch a ride with Arthur," I said. "I'll just go down and get in the backseat a few minutes before he's ready to leave. He won't know the difference."

In the thirty-one years since Arthur entered medical school, I could not begin to count the number of times he had mentioned how appalled I would be if I had to bear witness to his entire day. It was a blatant plea for sympathy, and it was sympathy I was happy to give him. I knew he worked hard, impossibly hard, but still, I couldn't help but feel there was some vague accusation in his request as well, like I didn't really understand what hard work was or I didn't fully appreciate all that he did on our behalf. It was something I became especially sensitive to after my own professional life was squeezed down to an occasional drip. "I wish you could just watch one entire day," he'd say to me. "You'd probably run screaming after an hour." How many times did I say, "Yes! Okay! I'd love to go. It's national Take Your Wife to Work Day. Show me how it's done." But of course it was the kind of thing you say, not the kind of thing you actually do. If the problem with Arthur's days was that they were too busy, then bringing me along was hardly going to make things easier. I would be in his way. There would be all the introductions to make. I could picture his nurse Mary pushing me into a supply closet and locking the door.

But as an invisible wife there was a real opportunity, and in some sense it was even better that he wouldn't know I had been there. "You're not going to do anything, to fix anything," Irene said as she drove me to the office. "You're just going to bear witness to his life. I think sometimes that's the greatest gift we can give one another."

"It's true," I said. "It happens to be the exact thing I'm missing from Arthur these days." I wriggled out of my clothes and rolled them into a ball, which I then pushed under the front seat.

"You first have to be willing to give what you want to get," Irene said. Irene changed lanes without checking her rearview mirror and I heard the sound of horns and screeching tires behind us. She was a beautiful soul and a terrible driver. What a thought, being in a car accident while invisible. Would they never find me? Would they tow me out to the junkyard and leave me there in the car? I shuddered.

"Here we are!" Irene said. "Now if this doesn't work out just call me and I'll come and pick you up. Do you have your cell phone?"

"You've got to go out there with nothing," I said, opening my hands. "That's the only way it works."

"Oh, Clover," she said, her pale eyes blinking back tears. "That's beautiful. That's completely Zen."

"Drive home safe," I said, and closed the door.

Right from the start I was cheating. It was almost ten o'clock. Arthur had left the house a little after seven. He would have already made rounds at the hospital, returned a spate of phone calls, met with the pretty drug reps who encouraged him to push their niacins, their allergy tablets, their Ritalin. On top of all that he had probably seen maybe six or eight patients. He was probably halfway to exhausted while I had spent my morning perfecting my triangle pose. I pushed the elevator button. I decided if there was something important I felt like I was missing I could always come back tomorrow morning.

There were seven pediatricians in Arthur's group, five men and two women, and of the seven Arthur was the second oldest. Bill, the oldest, was winding down. He didn't see new patients anymore, come in on Fridays, or take a rotation of weekend call (an unimaginable luxury as far as I was concerned). He had handed over the reins of the group to Arthur, though with only seven members I never thought that was asking so much. What did they talk about at their monthly meetings anyway? Whether or not to upgrade the quality of the toys in the toy box? Whether handing out Tootsie Pops after immunizations and booster shots promoted tooth decay and obesity? We would all have a

party together at Christmas with the nurses and the recep-
tionists and the women in billing. They were Arthur's other
family, the same way the newspaper people had been my
other family. That had been the thing I'd missed most of all
about working.

When I opened the door to the waiting room I found
myself in the midst of barely controlled chaos. While I
will admit my first impulse was to hustle straight back to
Arthur's office, I decided I would do well to prop myself
up against the wall for a couple of minutes and observe.
It made me feel like a journalist again, undercover as no
one had ever been undercover before. The waiting room
was, after all, part of the experience. While there were
big chairs and little chairs and very tiny chairs circling the
room, nearly all of them were empty. Children were careen-
ing all over the floor. I couldn't distinguish the sick from
the well. They were running fire trucks in circles while adding in the wailing noise of sirens themselves, scampering
in the front door and out the back door of a plastic castle,
rolling and tumbling and turning the pages in picture books
so fast that the pages sailed across the room. I imagined
the germs colliding, the impetigo bumping into the sore
throat who pushed over the earache who sat on the one
who was only there for an annual checkup. It was easy to
picture them on a school bus soon enough. Their mothers
chased them helplessly, and then gave up to talk to other
mothers.

Jeannine, who was my favorite of all the nurses, opened

the door. She wore a blue smock covered in SpongeBob SquarePants. "Mr. Goldberg," she called in a cheerful voice.

Mr. Goldberg, who was all of three years old, had an instant before been marching a dinosaur across the floor. Now he sat down and began to cry. His mother, greatly pregnant, leaned over and heaved the boy up with one arm and carried him.

"Max!" Jeannine said. "Aren't you glad to see me?"

Max wailed. "He isn't feeling well," his mother said.

I slipped into the hall behind them. In fact Max was very flushed and I reached over without thinking and touched his bright hot forehead. At the brush of my cool hand the boy was so startled that he forgot to finish crying but left his mouth hanging open in wonder.

"There you go!" Jeannine said cheerfully.

We were just rounding a corner when I saw Arthur standing at the nurses' station. His back was to us and he appeared to be looking at a chart. His lab coat was crisp and white and he was holding a big baby, a girl of maybe one, somewhat carelessly on his hip. She was looking at him with love and concentration. Clearly she did not feel well, and clearly in the arm of my husband she felt better, and so she hung there quietly and let him do his work, comforted by his proximity and the clean, starchy smell of his coat. Just like that my eyes filled up with tears and I blinked them back. Did everybody fall in love with him or was it just me? Arthur had given up running years ago and he ate pimento cheese sandwiches every day for lunch. Around his eyes he wore the look of the perpetually exhausted, yet he shone like the sun, the center of a small, specific solar system that spun around him all the days and nights. He turned and whispered something in the child's ear and then handed her back to her mother, a pretty redheaded girl who looked to be all of twenty.

"Dr. Hobart," Mary said, guiding him on. "Room five."

Mary had been with Arthur for ten years and without her, he had said so many times, he would probably manage to see about five patients a day. She was younger than I was and prettier, though it was impossible to think of her as either pretty or young. She was the harness and the plow, Arthur was always the mule. She took the chart from his hand, handed him another chart, and pointed to the door marked five. At every moment the telephone was ringing. Pam, the third nurse, answered, put someone on hold, and answered again, put them on hold, went back to the first call. Jeannine, having deposited the Goldbergs in room four, picked up another line and asked what she could do to help. Suddenly the redhead and the baby were gone and I was dashing down the hall to slip into room five before Mary closed the door on me.

There on the high exam table, atop a sheet of white paper, sat a twelve-year-old boy with thick brown curls brushed back from his forehead. He was a boy who looked like a player, a boy who could catch and throw and run. Maybe there was something wrong with his elbow. Behind him his mother was standing, her arms folded across her chest. The room was small and with Arthur and Mary and the mother and the boy I had to press myself into the corner near the sink.

"How are you doing today, Owen?" Arthur said.

"Still wetting the bed," the mother said flatly. Owen kept his eyes fixed forward, his fists pressed between his knees.

"A lot of people do," Arthur said. He put his hand on the boy's shoulder and gave it a squeeze. "We're going to run a few tests is all. Figure out what the problem is."

"The problem is he won't get up in the night," his mother said.

"That can be part of the problem," Arthur said to her sympathetically. "Would it be all right if Owen and I talked for a minute about this by ourselves?"

The mother sighed and held out her hands. "Have at it. I hope you'll have more luck with him than I do."

Mary opened the door and the mother made her exit, but when she closed the door Arthur looked at her. "You too," he said. "Just a minute."

Mary gave him a small frown. Once she was out of the room it was nearly impossible for her to keep him moving forward in a straight line. Arthur gave her a very small nod, which told her he understood and he wouldn't be forever. It was as if he were gently pushing her out. When finally she was gone he waited for the door to click before turning back to Owen.

"The Cardinals," he said gravely. "Do you think there's any hope for the play-offs?"

To make a sweeping generalization, the children would all be fine. With or without medical treatment they would survive the things that ailed them. It was the mothers who needed to be seen. Throughout the day they leaned forward and held Arthur's wrist. When he was finished examining their child they turned that child upside down to show my husband one more freckle, a fingernail that was perhaps less than lovely. They held up the daughter and asked if her knees were perfectly even. They stretched out the son, a mere infant, and commented that he had no neck, as if this could be a condition that required emergency surgery. Through it all, Arthur was patient. He put his glasses on and gave serious consideration to every bump. He listened to every story about the child who kept getting up in the night and crawling into the parents' bed. He leaned forward, nodded, tapped the shin gently with a small silver hammer to show them how normally the foot jumped. He soothed the mothers with his intelligent consideration of their nattering madness. Honestly, the man was a god.

Every five minutes Mary knocked on the door like a mad theater director. "Dr. Hobart, you have a call." "Dr. Hobart, a Dr. Jenkins needs to speak to you." "Dr. Hobart, we have a situation in the waiting room." And every time he politely extricated himself from the crisis at hand to go and attend to the crisis that was eight feet away, then he cycled back without losing his place in the sentence he was speaking or listening to. It went on and on and on. One of the other doctors grabbed him in the hall, waving an X-ray in his

had done something wrong, that they had ruined everything, until I wanted to scream, *Leave him alone!* Oh, Arthur, why didn't you tell me it was like this? Is it really like this every day? We could sell the house. I could get a job at Macy's. No one should have to work like this.

A child named Asa with straight black hair and pale blue eyes attached herself to both of his legs, making Arthur a tree trunk. The last patient was scheduled for four o' clock. The last patient was seen at five thirty. The mothers grumbled to the nurses, there would be traffic now, and what about dinner? Did they think it was fair that people with small sick children should be made to wait? The nurses apologized. Mary apologized. "It was a very busy day," she said, not explaining that in fact all of them were exactly the same, only some were worse.

"If he doesn't have time to see all these patients, then he shouldn't schedule them," one mother said in a voice sharp with reprimand, a voice that made me sorry for her child.

The charts were picked up. The toys were picked up, wiped off, returned to the bin in the waiting room. The nurses straightened up the rooms, washed their hands. One by one they stuck their heads into his office. "Good night, Dr. Hobart."

He said good night three times. I was lying on the floor beneath his desk where no one would step on me. My head was empty of thoughts. I was too tired to think. Instead I replayed the faces of the children. I saw them like crayons crowded into a box, all of them standing up next to one another very straight. It was impossible to try and consider each one separately.

While I lay there Arthur dictated letters, made notes in every chart, called other doctors, attended to every detail that his day had not allowed. "Isn't there someone you could hire to do all this?" I wanted to ask him. "Couldn't I come over at night and do this for you?" Finally I got up and went and stood behind his shoulder. I ached. I wondered if I had caught something awful. There was a line drawn through the name of every person on his list of people to call and there was only one chart left. It wasn't very late. After all of this, Arthur would be coming home early. And so I blew him a kiss and went downstairs and through the parking garage to the space with his name on it. But all four of the Acura's doors were locked. Arthur believed in locking the car, a habit I had never picked up. I waited, looked around. Even if no one could see me there, I don't like parking garages. I decided to go back upstairs. Maybe I could find his keys, go and unlock the car, then bring the keys back up. I was working through the complicated scenarios when I went back to Arthur's office. He was still at his desk but now the computer was on. He was looking at a website with bicycles. Bicycles? Did Arthur want a bicycle? This was news to me, but I made a mental note of the make and model he seemed to admire. Christmas was not too far off, as the decorations in the mall had reminded me, and Arthur was impossible to buy for. Maybe he wanted a bicycle because he wanted to exercise more. He wanted to do something for himself. He moved the mouse around and clicked. Up came a picture of a boat. It was a sailboat, and as he scrolled down, it was pages and pages of sailboats. Arthur had sailed with his father when he was a boy, and one summer between his sophomore and junior years of college he crewed on a boat that went down to Bermuda. It was a story he liked to tell. "One day," he often said, "we'll get a boat, the two of us, and we'll go to Bermuda. Maybe we'll get a bigger boat and take the kids." For a long time I would tell him how I got seasick, how I wasn't keen on confinement or long-term exposure to sun, but after a while I got it. It wasn't about a boat. It was about thinking about a boat. Then he switched the screen to planes and watched a few YouTube videos of aerobatics, stomach-plummeting spins and dives. He sat there in his white coat and watched the planes turn upside down and right side up, over and over again. That was when I got it. He wasn't coming home for a long time.

I went down the hall and called Irene from the phone at the front desk. "I think I'm going to need that ride," I said.

I got home and took a hot shower. I felt like I was crawling with germs. I put on some jeans and a sweater and ran back downstairs to heat up some stew I had made the night before. Red was bouncing around my ankles like he was on a trampoline he couldn't get off of.

"He isn't used to you being gone all day," Nick said.

"I know. The time just got away from me."

"But your car was here, and you didn't have your cell phone on."

I looked up at him. "Your grandmother picked me up, and you know I never know where my phone is. Did something happen?"

Nick pointed up at the ceiling. "Evie's home. She's a disaster. She said her boyfriend broke up with her, Vlad or whatever his name is. She says she's dropping out of school, that she won't go back."

"What did you tell her?" It was impossible that Evie would come home now. If Vlad had actually left her she would require more patience and compassion than Mother Teresa possessed, much less her own mother.

"I reminded her that Ohio State was playing Iowa a week from Saturday at home, and if she was going to be something as stupid as a cheerleader, then she needed to get her butt back to school and start practicing."

"Wow, Nick. Well done."

"It's not like I said that when she walked in the door but she's been crying *all day.* I tried to call Dad but that witch Mary answered the phone and she wouldn't let me talk to him. He's got to do something about her."

I saw the lights of Arthur's car in the driveway, and, as if on cue, my beautiful waif of a daughter stumbled down the stairs in a tiny Ohio State T-shirt and a pair of gray sweatpants with the word OHIO emblazoned across her rear end.

"Mommy," she wailed, and fell into my arms, the tiny rack of her shoulders shuddering against my chest.

"Home again," Arthur said brightly at the door, and Evie, who always was a daddy's girl, made a perfect pivot out of my arms and fell against her father's chest.

eight

"Hi, I'm Clover Hobart, and I'm an invisible woman."

"Hi, Clover!"

I waved my Kleenex at the group and they waved their Kleenex back at me. "It's been a really hard week. Just knowing that you're out there, that I have other invisible women that I can call, well, that's really been a help to me. I don't mean to say it's all bad. Lila Robinson and I had a real adventure spending the day in high school. Is Lila here?"

A Kleenex flapped lightly from the other side of the circle. "Right here."

"Have you gone back again?"

"Every day," she said. "And you're right, I'm already making a big difference. Disruptive conduct reports are pretty much down to zero. I've busted up incidences of cheating and bullying, thwarted some minor drug deals in which I made the kids flush the pot down the toilets themselves. I think I've done more for that school in the past five days than I did in thirty years. Each day I write down everything I've done and I leave it on the principal's desk. In another couple of weeks I'm going to ask for my job back."

This news was met with enthusiastic applause.

Lila hushed the group so that she could go on. "I've got to thank Clover here for telling me to stop feeling sorry for myself and get back to work. She hasn't been invisible very long but she knows how to jump in there and get things done. And thanks to Laura Worthington, too. Laura gave me the great advice about the importance of documenting what I was doing."

More applause, and another Kleenex wave from someone I assumed was Laura.

"You would have gone back to school without me," I said. "You're a natural. Anyway, I'm glad I could be helpful to someone else because I'm not doing nearly as good a job with my own life. I went to spend the day with my husband at work and I felt completely overwhelmed by all the pressure he has on him and I have no idea how to help him. Then when I came home my daughter, Evie, was there. She says she's dropped out of college because her boyfriend has broken up with her."

Audible groans.

"I know. She's twenty years old! Who cares if your boyfriend breaks up with you when you're twenty? She should probably send him a thank-you note. She's been home for three days now. All she does is cry and text."

"Does she know you're invisible?" someone asked. I thought it was the group leader, Jo Ellen.

The very thought forced an involuntary burble of laughter up my throat. "Evie is a sweet girl but she wouldn't notice if the house was on fire. The extent to which she never lifts her eyes from her iPhone cannot be overemphasized. I actually worry about her poor little thumbs."

"Is the boyfriend still texting her?" There was Alice. She was sitting right next to me.

"Constantly. I can remember when I was visible I was so curious about her texts. What could these kids possibly be discussing at such length? Now that I can just stand over her shoulder and read them all day I have to say I have never encountered anything so boring in my entire life. They are literally saying nothing over and over again for hours on end." I sighed and shook my head. "This isn't what I wanted to talk about. Evie and Vlad have broken up, Evie's dropped out of school, she cries, they text. Chances are she'll pull it together and go back by the end of the week, at least that's what Nick tells me. He also figured out that this is her fall break so dropping out of school doesn't have quite the same punch just yet."

"Who's Nick?" a voice asked.

"My son. He graduated from college two years ago but he's living at home again and looking for a job."

More groans.

I felt like I was just about to make my point when the big double doors to the Magnolia Room opened and an older Filipino woman, not the one from last week, came in and closed the door behind her. Before we even had time to drop our Kleenex she pulled a chair out from the circle. I didn't know who was sitting in it but I saw the Kleenex dart up, and then the woman sat down, removing a sandwich and a cell phone from her pocket. Once she'd peeled back the plastic wrap from the sandwich and taken a bite, she punched in a number and began a loud conversation in a language I did not understand. Whoever was on the other end of the line couldn't get a word in edgewise. The invisible women waited patiently, as patience is our particular virtue, but after a while I started to wonder how long this woman's break was. The conversation, if you could call it that, appeared to be endless.

"Do you think she would hear us if we kept on talking?" Alice said.

We waited, but no, she didn't seem to hear. The Magnolia Room was enormous, but because of its enormity it was also the room that was the most consistently available.

"Let's just move our chairs," Jo Ellen said. And so we got up and dragged our chairs to the other side of the room, reassembling our circle far away from the caller, who didn't seem to notice the furniture moving away on its own.

"That's better," Jo Ellen said. "Not perfect, but better. Clover, I believe you were talking."

Over a one-sided conversation in Filipino I began again. "What I wanted to say is that having Evie home is really teaching me something about invisibility. She's invisibility's polar opposite. She's the most visible creature on the planet. Even I can't stop staring at her. It's as if she's walking under a klieg light every minute of the day and you can't help notice every single thing about her, the length of her eyelashes, the shadow under her collarbone. She twists her hair up with one hand and jams a pencil through it with the other and I swear to you a team of New York stylists could not create anything so flawless."

"So what's wrong with this Vlad?" Alice asked. "Assuming she's a nice girl, why did he dump her?"

"From what I can piece together from his texts it's all too terrifying for him. He's a kid himself, and a kid named Vlad on top of that. He's afraid she's going to leave him. All of his friends are teasing him. All of his friends are hitting on her. Everywhere she goes people turn around and stare. We go to the grocery store and people ask her questions: Where did you get that lip gloss? What color is your nail polish? Frankly, even her grief seems to make her more beautiful. She's turned this extraordinary combination of pale and flushed. She looks like the inside of a seashell."

"So you have a pretty daughter," Jo Ellen said flatly. "I'm sure we're all happy for you."

"Hey," Lila said. "She's trying to make a point here."

I closed my eyes, though against what view it would have been difficult to say. I listened to the continuing drone of conversation from across the room. It made a shelter of white noise. I opened my eyes to our nothingness, our Kleenex, our empty chairs. "I have a pretty daughter, I do. She's like a bonfire on the darkest night of the year, a bonfire on a prairie in a snowstorm. You can't help yourself, you're going to turn in her direction, and she's doing nothing to make this happen. She's wearing sweatpants and she isn't bathing very much and nothing decreases the light she's putting out, and that's what I keep thinking about: where's the light we're putting out? Part of what's so painful about being invisible is that I realize now how long it's been going on, how long it's been since anyone on the street turned around and looked at me, how long it's been since my husband really looked at me, or since I looked at myself. I mean honestly, I don't even know how long I was invisible before I noticed. But if Evie stopped turning up, it would be like a power outage in Manhattan."

"The beautiful are seen and the less than beautiful aren't seen," Laura Worthington said. Hers was the voice of experience. "That's the way of the world."

"Yes," I said. "Right. But there's more to it than beauty. Beauty is the easy part. We relied on it, we got used to it, and then when it faded we faded along with it. But what I see in Evie is this light, this bright life, and even though it's all tied up in beauty for her it doesn't have to be for us. We've got to start thinking about what makes us light. Simply put, invisible women have to work a lot harder to be seen. We don't have our youth. We don't have the clothes or the jewelry to get a little flash."

"Jewelry doesn't work," Lila said.

"So we've got to figure out who we are. We've got to stop standing around in the corner wondering if anybody is missing us. We have to find our light so people still know that we're here. Lila found it. She went back to school. Pretty soon they're going to realize they can't make the place work without an invisible woman. Even if they can't see her, her light is going to be everywhere."

And then abruptly, as far as those of us who did not speak Filipino could tell, the woman across the room snapped her cell phone shut, threw away her piece of plastic wrap, and left the room without a glance in our direction.

"So, Clover," Patty Sanchez said. "What's your light?"

I looked at my Kleenex floating in the place just above where my knees should be. "I don't know yet," I said. "But I'm working on it."

When I got home no one was there, not even Red. I was standing in the kitchen shaking a box of dog biscuits and feeling the smallest edge of panic when my cell phone buzzed in my pocket—a text from Evie.

KEMPTONS, it said, answering the question I had not asked.

So everything was fine. I trusted Gilda to look after the dog. I barely trusted the children to look after themselves.

Having just come in from a meeting I was fully dressed. I did think it was important to be dressed while driving. Still, I put on a big bunchy scarf that had been a failed experiment from last year's brief knitting phase. Ever since the incident with the bathrobe, I tended toward greater coverage when I was with Gilda.

Benny met me at the door and gave a couple of modest sniffs at the passing air after letting me in. I wish I could say he was on to me but I could see in his confused little eyes that he was nowhere close to putting the pieces together. "Why aren't you in school?" I said suspiciously.

"Fall break," he whispered, and then motioned with his hand that I should follow him. Benny was wearing his socks without shoes and he made an effort to be very, very quiet as he walked. In the den I found Gilda sitting on the couch, Evie asleep with her head in Gilda's lap, Gilda with her hand in Evie's tumble of golden hair. Across from her Miller sat in a chair and silently watched as if this were a particularly riveting play that had just arrived at its heart-stopping final act. Benny took up the chair beside his brother and resumed his watching as well. Red, who was on the couch near Evie's feet, raised his head and, looking at me, gave his tail a single, definitive thump of greeting and then he put his head back on his paws.

"She just now fell asleep," Gilda whispered.

Miller glanced up in my direction, checking to make

sure I had no intention of waking her or, worse yet, taking her away. "She's been crying," he said, or I think that's what he said. His voice was so quiet I was practically lip reading, a favor that was never returned for invisible women.

I sat down on an ottoman and joined the audience for my sleeping daughter. Truly she was something to behold. With her face clean of makeup (she didn't bother with it when there was so much crying to do) and untroubled by dreams, she looked closer to twelve than to twenty. In fact, it was as if I were looking at the child she had been not so long ago, falling asleep across the backseats of so many cars. With her overlarge eyes and round rosebud mouth and thick blond eyebrows arched into wings, she was the fairest of all the Dickens heroines, Estella and little Nell and the beautiful, foolish Dora, at least that's what I was thinking when her phone began to vibrate in her little pink fist. She let out a generic exclamation—*ah!* or *oh!*—and sat straight up, drawing her feet in so fast she knocked Red off the couch.

"Is it him?" Gilda asked, pulling her glasses off the top of her head and down to her nose so she could read along.

Evie held up her iPhone and commenced her crying again, although this crying was clearly of a different order, the diamond-bright tears of joy. "He's coming! He says he's in the car. He's on the interstate now!" She turned and fell into Gilda. "He's coming here!"

Miller and Benny both leaned back, disgusted. The play had taken an unimaginable turn. They were finished. "I've got homework," Benny said.

"On the first day of break?" Gilda asked.

"I'm going to the coffee shop," Miller said. "See if Nick has found us a job."

"He's texting on the interstate?" I said. "While he's driving?"

"I have to wash my hair!" Evie's hand shot up to the extravagant mess of her head. "He didn't say what time he left! He didn't say what time he was going to be here!"

"Well," Gilda said, "he texted you ten minutes ago to say he wasn't coming, so I think you can assume he just left."

"What if he changes his mind? What if he doesn't come?"

"Then you will be exactly as you are now except with clean hair," I said.

Evie started to say something sharp, I saw the look cross her face, though just as quickly she thought it through. She pressed her hands across her Ohio State T-shirt. "I should go get something to wear, something pretty. I only came home with sweatpants."

"Don't kill him," Gilda said. "Washing your hair is plenty. He's not driving down here to see your wardrobe."

The lovely yellow head of my daughter drooped, an unwatered daisy. "I look so awful," she said, and then she did the most remarkable thing—she picked up a hank of her own hair and dried her tears.

"Take the car," I said, knowing that in the end I would give in anyway and wanting to just jump ahead. "The keys are on the kitchen counter."

Evie shook her head, sniffled. "You have to come with

me. I can't go by myself. I'm too upset. I wouldn't know what to get." She turned and took Gilda's hand. "You'll come with us, won't you?" Her phone buzzed again and she dropped Gilda's hand and started texting again.

"The boy?" Gilda asked.

Evie shook her head. "It's Niki." Her thumbs were flying. "It's about cheerleading practice."

Gilda and I looked at each other, which is to say I looked at her and she looked above my scarf. She shrugged, then nodded. "Okay," she said. "But I'm going to drive."

I knew this drill, and I knew that cash was the essential element. For however much Evie enjoyed my company and my input on how different outfits complimented her appearance, I also knew she was broke. The invitation to join her was not without agenda. To send a pretty girl off to the mall with a mother's credit card was ruinous, unthinkable. I made it a point not to create scenarios in which my children were bound to fail. A set amount of cash at the beginning of such expeditions had been my traditional answer for avoiding meltdowns in J. Crew later in the day. It also meant that if at some point along the way my stamina failed me I could leave her there with the money and pick her up with her shopping bags later on.

"I need to go to the bank," I said to Gilda once the three of us were in the car.

Had I been driving, no doubt the day would have turned out differently. I would have cashed a check at the drive-in window or gone to the ATM machine. But as luck would have it, Gilda needed to go to the bank as well—her bank, which was not my bank—and she needed to go inside, and since it was cold and Evie hadn't worn a coat (coats were viewed as burdensome on shopping expeditions) she came in too. We stood at an island desk in the center of the bank, its glass top covering a multitude of transactional choices— slips for savings withdrawals and checking deposits and payments of loans. I wrote out a check for Gilda to cash and Gilda tallied up a small stack of checks to deposit while Evie plunked herself down in a chair and proceeded to text the world the news of Vlad's return. Because my chore was easier than either of theirs, I took a moment to look around. It was a pretty bank, much nicer than mine, with a brass chandelier stretching out above our heads and marble floors and a cherrywood counter behind which a multitude of tellers were ready and waiting to serve the dozen or so customers who were standing in line. There was a sleepy-looking security guard and four glass-fronted offices where bankers sat at desks and discussed mortgages and annuities with clients who listened and nodded.

In truth, invisibility had done a great deal to heighten my powers of observation. Now that I realized how shameless people were in all they did not see, I made it a point to see more myself. Irene would have said this was part of the lesson of my journey. There was a too-thin teller in her fifties, her oversized glasses perching on the tip of her nose while she counted and recounted a pile of money. There was a man in a suit, a nicer suit than all the others, who was probably the manager, as he kept opening the glass doors of the glass offices and dispatching a sentence here and there. There was a mother of two small boys who was trying very hard to keep them from hanging on the velvet ropes that guided the lines to the tellers, but the ropes were irresistible to boys and no matter how desperately she tried to make them be good they could not oblige. There was a man in jeans with his hands buried deep in the pockets of his puffy blue jacket, his mouth set in a straight line, as if he was bracing himself for the news that his account was overdrawn, or at least that's what I was thinking about him until he pulled a gun out of his pocket and at the same moment stepped behind the guard and pulled his gun out of the holster as easily as you could snatch a toy away from a child. He held up two guns.

"Everybody down!" he said, the force of his voice so enormous it could have knocked us to the floor by itself. We fell without thought, the entire room in perfectly synchronized obedience. The man's eyes went to Evie of course, where else could they go, and he saw that she was still texting, no doubt recording the moment as it happened. He stormed toward her and pointed his gun at my daughter's bright head as he snatched her phone from her hands. He might as well have ripped out her heart the way she screamed. He screamed at her in reply, "No phones! Hands flat out on the floor in front of you. Everybody! Hands out!"

What I heard at that moment was Arthur's voice. "Clover!" he said as he held me that night after I told him about the man in the parking lot. "For all you knew that man had a gun."

It is an impractical superpower that requires both an exit to change clothes and then a reentrance to the scene of the ongoing crime. Who has time to change? I could not leave to find a phone booth or make my way back to the bat cave, but oh, did I have a lifetime of experience getting out of my clothes. While the puffy-jacket bandit was making his way to the tellers I was already out of my pants and shoes and socks. Flat on my back I was twisting out of my top.

"What are you *doing?*" Gilda hissed.

"I'm saving the day," I said. Sweater, jacket, big, failed scarf, I was wriggling free of all of them. I was on my feet. It was my moment. It was the revenge of all invisible women.

"Clover," Gilda said, her voice forceful and low. "Your bra."

I looked down and saw a particularly ratty beige Maidenform bra floating in space, dangerous in how it all but drew a bull's-eye over my heart. I reached behind me and fumbled with the hook and eye. It gave me a split second of trouble that I didn't need, as now I saw a second man, younger and equally armed, standing near the door, and he was watching the bra, having no idea what it was about. Evie was back to her weeping and Gilda was craning her head around. I threw down the last of my undergarments.

My superpower was my absence, nothing else. Shoot me and I assume I'd be as dead as anyone. But while the people who could be seen were rightfully paralyzed by fear (it was easy to shoot what can be seen, especially when it was lying still on the floor right at your feet), invisibility allowed me to bypass fear and progress straight to rage. Enough of being stolen from! Enough of being told to shut up and get down! Enough of anyone terrorizing my daughter, my friend, these strangers, the poor skinny teller who with trembling hands was now being forced to lift the full tills out of every cash drawer. I reached around the puffy-jacket man, who, I realized once he was in my arms, was wearing the coat to make himself appear bigger than he was, and took a gun out of each of his hands. There was nothing tricky about it. The grips were wet from the sweat of his palms and they slipped out as if they were oiled. Quickly, quickly, because no one likes the part where guns seem to be flying through the air, I gave one to the guard and one to the man in the nicer suit. The boy at the door, seeing that the tides of fortune were shifting, turned to make a run for it. I took his gun as well. I didn't want to capture him, capturing was not in my job description, but I would have hated to see him hurt someone on his way out. That third gun I gave to Gilda. I put it under her hand that was spread out flat on the floor.

"I don't want a gun," she hissed. The security guard had handcuffed puffy-jacket's arms behind his back and was leading him to a glass office. The manager, dazed and now armed, was helping the clientele up from the floor.

"It's good for you," I said. "Take responsibility." I crouched down beside her on the floor. "Listen, if it's okay I'm going to go wait in the car. I don't want to try and explain all this."

"Sure," Gilda said, sitting up tentatively. "You did a great job."

Evie was searching around for her phone. I was trying to push my clothes together into a discreet pile and roll them into my jacket. When the police burst in I saw my chance and made a break for it through the open door, my bunched-up clothing tucked beneath my arm like a cowboy's bedroll. I would ride right out of town and no one would miss me. Nobody but Gilda knew I had saved the day, that Clover Hobart was that masked man.

nine

*I*t turned out to be a long, long wait in the car, plenty of time for me to get dressed again and wonder if there was some order in the universe. After all, suburban bank robberies were hardly common fare in this day and age. I had made it fifty-four years without ever having stumbled into one. So was this my newfound luck or lack of luck? In truth, I felt pretty good as I silently replayed the movie in my mind. A surge of adrenaline was still pumping through my invisible veins. I used to wonder what the chances were that banks would so often be robbed in front of Superman, so many purses snatched outside the diner where Spider-Man drank his coffee. But now I knew they must have gone looking for trouble. Trouble, it turned out, felt good. It was a kick and a half to see justice prevail, and only mildly disappointing that no one would ever know that you were the one who made it happen. I could picture a world in which I wandered through the roughest bars at night, looking for people to set straight. Then again, that's what Lila and I had done all day in the high school and that had been nothing but exhausting. Maybe what made it fun was the sheer surprise of it all.

When Gilda and Evie finally arrived they were visible wrecks. Gilda came around to the passenger side and handed me the keys. "You drive," she said.

"How did you get out to the car?" Evie said, collapsing across the backseat. "We looked for you everywhere."

"I just walked out. I thought you were both behind me. Then the police closed the building and that was that."

"Well, you were smart," Gilda said. "I found the crime scene more taxing than the crime. They kept us forever. They wanted to know what I was doing with a gun."

"So what did you tell them?"

"I told them the truth," Gilda said pointedly. "I had my head down, I didn't see what happened, and the next thing I knew a gun came skidding across the floor in my direction. I caught it, that's all. I was lucky it didn't hit me in the head."

"I would say we were all pretty lucky," I said, and I meant

it. There was no way things could have been better and almost every way in which they could have been worse.

"But they wouldn't give me back my phone!" Evie said. "They found it right in the guy's pocket but they said they had to take it in as part of the evidence. I mean, it's pink and it says *Evie* on the back of it. Of course it's mine! They said even if it was my phone he might have used it to make calls. Like, duh, when did he have time to make calls while he was robbing the stupid bank? They wouldn't even let me check my messages! Now I don't know when Vlad is coming or even if he's coming. He may have broken up with me again."

I dug my phone out of my purse with one hand and tossed it over the seat. "Here," I said. "Text your heart out."

Evie looked at my phone and gasped. "There are only numbers on your phone."

"The letters are underneath the numbers," I said. "Just like the old days. It just takes a little longer."

"I can't believe you use this."

"Your father and I are trying to save money so our children can get an education."

But at the mention of saving money, Evie turned and looked out the back window at the shopping complex that was receding behind us. "I thought we were going to the mall," she said in a very small voice.

"No!" Gilda and I said together.

She turned and slumped down in her seat. "Now I don't have a phone and I don't have an outfit," she said, though mostly to herself. "Great outing. I should have just stayed home."

"How about this?" I said. "'Mom! Gilda! We weren't shot by a crazed bank robber. How exciting is that!'"

"He didn't look so crazed," Evie said petulantly.

"He put a gun to your head!" Gilda screamed. "Clover, pull the car over so I can climb back there and hit your child."

I thought about it, I really did, but I just wanted so badly to get home.

As soon as I pulled into Gilda's driveway Evie was out of the car and running across the street so that she could get to work on her grooming. I had reminded her that she hadn't taken every article of clothing she owned to college, such a thing would never have been possible, so surely she could find something in her closet that Vlad had never seen before. Once she was gone, Gilda and I sunk down in our seats. For a long time we were quiet, just watching the lines of the bare branches hatching up the gray clouds behind them.

"Cup of tea?" I asked finally.

"Bottle of merlot?" she replied.

"I don't think I should drink. I'm really tired all of a sudden." So tired, in fact, that sleeping in the car for just a minute didn't strike me as a bad idea.

"She never noticed," Gilda said, her voice all hollow.

"Noticed what?"

"You, what you did. How you risked your life to save all

of us. That you're invisible. She didn't notice any of it." My friend shook her head sadly. "I love that girl but I don't know how you put up with it, Clover. If I were you I'd be pretty depressed right now."

I shrugged and the shoulders of my jacket went up, then down. "Actually, I'm feeling pretty good. I'm starting to see the benefits of my condition. Maybe I was meant to fight crime. That wouldn't be such a bad outcome to all of this. Anyway, we didn't have to take Evie shopping."

"When you put it that way I can see your point." We sat quietly for a minute. Neither one of us had enough energy to open our car door. "Clover?"

"Right here," I said.

"Do you remember the winter we went to Florida? When you first moved into the neighborhood, when we were first friends?"

"Of course I remember Florida." We had gone to Fort Lauderdale and stayed in a Hyatt. We left our husbands alone with our children. From where we were sitting now it seemed like an impossible dream. "There was that guy in the bar who kept hitting on us." Not an attractive guy, but still, a guy.

"'Are you girls from Fort Lauderdale?'" Gilda said in a slurry voice.

"And you said, 'Listen, my friend and I only have two nights of vacation and we're not going to spend one of them being polite to you.' I remember thinking, there is a woman who knows how to take charge of life."

"But we didn't get two nights of vacation." Gilda was staring out the window looking like she had just that moment gotten bad news. "Benny got sick. Do you remember? Steve wanted me to come home."

"Well, that's motherhood. You do what you have to do. We still had a good time."

"He wasn't that sick," Gilda said.

"You didn't know it then." Arthur had taken Benny to the office for a culture. Was it strep? Not that it made any difference.

"The point is, we swore we'd go back every year. We drank a toast to it in the airport. We'd go back to Florida every winter—"

"Even if it was only for a night," I said. I remembered. We were drinking Salty Dogs.

"We didn't go back, Clover," Gilda said, turning to me. "Somebody tries to shoot you in a bank and you think about those things. I want to have my toenails painted and sit on the beach and read a stupid magazine. If that's what I'm asking for in the face of death, I have to say it doesn't strike me as a lot."

"I can't get my toenails painted anymore," I said. I thought of the poor pedicurist trying to find my toes and I started to laugh and then we both started to laugh.

"I wonder if you'd still have to use sunblock?"

"What if I tanned? I'd still be invisible but sort of beige."

"Like smog," Gilda sputtered and then poked my arm. "Promise me we'll go again when things have settled down."

"Promise," I said. "But we might not want to wait that long."

I walked in the door of my house and went straight to bed. All I wanted was a few minutes of sleep. It turned out that crime fighting, after the initial adrenaline rush wore off, was exhausting. But Evie kept waking me up to ask which of her adorable outfits she looked most adorable in.

"This?" she asked. She was wearing a pair of breathtakingly short shorts, some Uggs that looked like slouchy sweaters, and a tank top topped with a charcoal blazer with the sleeves rolled up. It was a compelling combination of coverage and nudity.

"Where did you get the blazer?" I asked. It was familiar to me and yet I wouldn't have pegged it as Evie's style.

"Nick's closet." She looked at herself in the mirror, then she turned around to scrutinize her backside. "It makes me look fat."

"That, my love, is not possible." I could barely keep my eyes open.

"Wait," she said, as if I had someplace to go. As soon as she was out of the room I pulled the covers over my head and went to sleep. It made her change of clothes seem like a magic trick because as far as I was concerned she had been gone exactly one second and now she was back again in a different outfit. She was poking my shoulder through the covers. "Mom?"

This time she was wearing a pink gingham-check shirt dress that buttoned up the front. It had been her favorite dress in high school and for one summer she had worn it at least three times a week. It was faded and soft looking and I wanted to scoop her up in my arms and make her take a nap with me. "You look so cute."

She turned to the mirror to confirm my assessment. "I hate it," she said.

"Even with a belt?" I asked hopefully.

She sat down on the edge of the bed and covered her face with her hands. "He isn't going to love me anymore. He probably isn't even coming. He probably just said he was coming because he knew I'd run around trying to decide what to wear when he knows I didn't pack when I left school and I don't have anything to wear."

"Really," I said. "He thinks about all of that?"

"You don't understand," she said, and then she paused for a long time as if trying to decide whether or not she wanted to make me understand. "I wasn't exactly nice."

I reached up and let my invisible hand disappear into the tangled corn silk of her hair. "So now he's coming and you have a chance to be exactly nice."

She picked up the corner of the sheet and wiped her face. "I'm going to change," she said.

"Change your personality but leave your outfit alone," I said. "You look terrific." As she was walking away I was thinking that I'd take being invisible over being twenty any day of the week. Poor Evie, it was as if she were a princess who couldn't decide which of her diamond tiaras to wear to the ball.

I had just fallen asleep again and was dreaming one of those mortifying dreams of childhood where you're at a party and you're the only one who's naked. Then suddenly the doorbell rang and Red exploded off the bed in a cacophony of frantic barking. I could hear Evie screaming as she ran down the stairs, "Vlad! Vlad!"

When I came down she was wearing her Ohio State sweatpants and her Ohio State T-shirt again. Clearly he had arrived in between outfits. After all the weeping and embracing and pleas for forgiveness had subsided, I shook his hand. Vlad was as tall as a tree, pale as a root, his great head bowed at the thought that he could ever have been so wrong. How could he have managed without her? His light green eyes were rimmed in red. He looked unfed, unrested, unwashed. I saw him bite his ragged lip slightly and give me a sad look. Clearly this breakup had wrung the life out of him.

"Vlad can stay in my room," Evie said, both of her hands encircling his left elbow. She did not give me time to raise my eyebrows, which I had planned on doing, not that anyone would have noticed. "I'll sleep in the den. He's too big for the couch."

I wanted to point out that the boy would not get a moment's rest on her ladybug sheets, though I could have also mentioned that Vlad had not been invited to spend the night. Still, even I could see that there would be no sending this enormous boy into the night to drive back to wherever he came from. "We'll work it out," I said, and went to the kitchen to make dinner.

I made a huge vat of pasta for dinner, adding in every last vegetable and hunk of cheese I could find. I was working on the assumption that certain desires I didn't want to think about were often sublimated with food. There was bread in the freezer, enough lettuce to pull together a salad. Arthur came home and Nick came home and they were both relieved to see Vlad, who had as recently as last night's dinner been referred to around our table as "Vlad the Cad" (though really, he could just as easily have been Howard the Coward or Tony the Phony). In truth, all anybody wanted was for Evie to stop crying, and after three long days of watching her weep we could all understand how a boyfriend might be tempted to dump her. At the table we raised a glass to reconciliation and good luck.

"Good luck!" we all called out together and clinked our glasses.

"Speaking of good luck," Arthur said. "Did you hear there was a bank robbery today at the First United Bank? Apparently the robber had some sort of a seizure right in the middle of the holdup and threw his guns across the room. They caught the guy and no one was hurt."

"Did we hear about it?" Evie said, twirling her spaghetti around her fork. "Daddy, we were *there*. Didn't Mom even call you?"

"Not that she could have gotten through," Nick said.

"What do you mean, you were there?" Vlad asked.

"You were driving by?" Arthur said.

"We were in the bank when it happened, me and Gilda and Mom. I can't believe she didn't tell you. There were so many other things going on. Daddy, the robber took my *phone*."

Arthur dropped his eyes to his plate, searching out an artichoke heart with his fork. "I don't understand what she's talking about."

I had to smile at his blanket unwillingness to see what was in front of him. "The girl means what she says. We were in the bank when it was robbed. It does seem a little impossible that I forgot to tell you."

"It does," Arthur said.

"The whole thing went by in about a minute," I said. "Maybe we have post-traumatic stress disorder."

"Then Vlad came," Evie said, reaching beside her to wrap her arm around the arm of her dinner companion. "The bank was like a million years ago."

Still, Arthur and Nick and Vlad wanted to hear every detail, and so we told them, Evie and I, splitting the narrative between us: we were going shopping, stopped by the bank, writing checks, sending texts, a sudden shout, *On the floor!* (Evie delivered that one with surprising gusto), then the gun, the loss of the beloved phone, and then, inexplicably, it was over. Everyone was very impressed that we were not afraid. They said how odd it was, the robber throwing his guns away.

"I think he had a change of heart," Evie said. "If he hadn't stolen my phone I would have thought he wasn't such a bad guy."

"It's a shame you aren't a reporter anymore," Nick said to me. "That's the kind of story that could get you back on the front page of the paper."

I looked at my son and the room wobbled slightly, the way it had that moment I first saw the gun. I was a reporter at a bank robbery. How had I not thought of that?

When finally the story had been told and retold to everyone's satisfaction and we were all finished eating, Arthur announced that he was sorry to leave good company but he had an early day tomorrow and he had to get to bed. Nick said he had promised to go over to Miller's to watch a basketball game, Evie said she had to go and straighten up her room (no doubt the floor was covered in clothes), and Vlad said he would like to wash the dishes. My family, just on the verge of scattering, stopped to stare at him.

"You don't need to do that," Evie said, graciously neglecting to mention that that was why they had me.

Vlad stood up and began stacking plates. His arms were nearly long enough to clear the entire table without moving from his spot. "I always wash the dishes," he said. "In my family we all have a job and that's my job."

"Marry him," Nick said to his sister, and, saying good night to the rest of us, was out the door.

While the rest of the Hobarts all disappeared, I picked up the glasses and followed Vlad into the kitchen. He put his stack of plates in the sink and reached behind me to shut the door. He waited a minute, making sure their footsteps had all retreated. "How long?" he said.

"How long what?" I asked him. I was thinking it was a question about Evie: How long had she cried for? How long had she missed him?

"How long have you been invisible?"

I turned to him, this giant boy. I was dumbstruck, gobsmacked. It was more surprising than the gun. "A month maybe." My voice was just a whisper. "Somewhere around a month."

"And none of them know?"

I shook my head. "No."

"I was going to say something to Evie but then I thought I shouldn't. If she had known, she would have told me. She sort of tells me everything."

For a minute I couldn't find my words and I thought, Now I am invisible and mute. I swallowed. "I appreciate you not telling her." He was just a kid and, I would have thought until about thirty seconds ago, a sort of average kid, who had figured out the thing that even the people who loved me most in the world had failed to grasp. "How did you know?"

"Well," he said, looking puzzled at my simplemindedness, "I can't see you."

"Sure, but no one can see me."

"And my mom's invisible."

"You're kidding me!"

"It's going on a year now. It took my dad almost two weeks to notice and she was so mad at him by the time he did that she wanted to get a divorce. I mean, from where I'm standing it looks like you're being really nice about this."

"I have my bad days," I said. "How long did it take you to notice your mom was gone?"

"I was away at school and so they called and told me on the phone. I mean, I guess I don't know what it's like to not be looking for it because when you know what to look for, it's like, just so obvious. I mean, you don't have a head. You'd think they'd catch on to that."

I had to agree. "You would."

He looked back at the closed door as if he imagined they were all standing outside listening. He lowered his voice. "So why don't you just tell them? Wouldn't it be better for everybody?"

"It would," I said. "I know it would. But after a while it just becomes a point of pride. You start to wonder just how far it can go."

He hit his forehead with his hand. "That's exactly what my mom said!"

"Are your parents okay now?"

He teetered his head back and forth. "Honestly? If you wouldn't mind my telling them about you I think it would really help a lot. We live on a farm, you know. We're sort of isolated. The town is real small, not like it is here. There aren't any other invisible women. I mean, we haven't seen them."

I leaned over and patted his hand. "You have your mom call me," I said. "If you can just hold off telling Evie for a little while I'll tell your mom anything she wants to know."

Vlad gave me a small smile of genuine happiness at the thought that he might have saved his own relationship and his parents' marriage in a single day. He turned on the water and started rinsing off the plates. "She'd really like that. I've changed my major to chemistry since this happened to her. I'm going premed. I'm going to figure this thing out. I know that might sound stupid to you, like I'm just talking, but I promise it's really important to me. A woman becomes invisible and nobody seems to care one way or the other. But it's my mom, you know, and now it's Evie's mom. I'm going to do something about it."

"I'd be very grateful," I said. There was a lump coming up in the back of my throat, a big, invisible lump.

"It was you who stopped that bank robbery today, wasn't it?"

Nothing got by this kid. I couldn't believe him. "It was me."

He nodded. "My mom has done some crazy stuff since she went invisible. It scares my dad to death. He's always saying she's gone fearless."

I started putting the plates in the dishwasher, thinking how glad I would be if Evie and Vlad eloped tonight, giving me an invisible in-law. "Yes," I said. "It's just like that."

ten

The first thing I did the next morning was call my editor at the paper, not an e-mail or a text, I actually picked up the phone. Right off the bat, Ed asked me what my angle was for next week's gardening column. "I've been thinking about mulching," he said.

"Forget the leaves," I said. "I've got news. I was at First United Bank yesterday."

"You went there after the robbery?" he said. I could hear his chair creak as he shifted his weight forward to sit up. Ed only sat up if he was interested.

"I was there *while* it was being robbed. I was on the floor."

"And you didn't think to call me until today?" His voice displayed a rare burst of emotion. "You should have called me while you were still on the floor."

"The bank robber wasn't letting us file stories," I said flatly.

"Clover, it's tomorrow already. This is a great pitch but you know it's a day late."

"Cut me a break here, Ed. I've been writing gardening columns and book reviews for years now. I've lost my sense of timeliness. At least let me write an op-ed. Let me write something about how long it's been since a bank was robbed in this city. I can make a link between bank robberies and the tight economy. I can talk about what it feels like to lie on a cold marble floor, to see the gun. You know this story has enough local interest to sustain two days of coverage. You could run it on the first page and sell papers off the stands."

There was a long pause. Ed was forty years old, he had three kids, he put in fourteen-hour days. Ed was interested in selling papers. It was how he kept his job. "Six hundred words. And it's in by three."

"Twelve hundred words," I said. "And I have until five."

"Eight hundred words, maybe nine hundred depending on how the layout goes. But I've got to have it by four. And talk about the robber. People are saying he just threw the guns away and nobody can figure that out. The public defender isn't letting him make a statement to the press but at least tell me what the whole thing looked like."

"Sold," I said.

I hung up the phone and for once was glad that no one could see me, the smile on my face was big enough to crack my head in half. In the years I had mourned the loss of a sustaining stream of book reviews and the job of being an editor myself, I had forgotten that I had once been a reporter. I'd been wasting my time trying to dream up interesting things that could be done with leftover poinsettias. In all my longing for a comeback, I had simply failed to remember the person I used to be.

Arthur had already gone to work, and Nick and Evie and Vlad were still asleep. If I was here when they woke up, I would spend the morning making pancakes and scrambling eggs. But I had fed and walked the dog, and as far as I was concerned everybody else was on their own. I dressed for maximum coverage, put my computer in a bag, and drove to the library.

If I had any problem it was keeping myself to nine hundred words. The minute I opened my computer I fell into typing. I was dying to write! Maybe it was a little odd to write a first-person account of how I lay trembling on the floor with the rest of the terrified patrons while the gunmen mysteriously threw their firearms in the air. It was the kind of thing that would have presented a problem to my journalistic sense of ethics when I was twenty-four, but at fifty-four it didn't even strike me as a speed bump. I sailed ahead. The truth, we realize as we get older, is a very complicated pastiche of feelings and facts, of what can and cannot be said. It's different for everyone. I read the piece over and then read it again. I polished, trimmed, improved my verbs. I checked my word count seventeen times, sighed, and pushed back from my desk. I knew I was completely and irrefutably finished but it was only eleven o'clock. If I turned it in now, Ed would think I wasn't working hard enough, and then he'd spend the rest of the day making me rewrite things that didn't need to be rewritten. I saved the file, went back to the Internet, and pulled up Dexter-White.

It was as if my mind had suddenly come to life. How could a drug company knowingly manufacture a series of drugs that, when taken in combination, rendered women invisible, and how could they fail to do anything about it? How was it that all along I had been seeing myself as a victim of the industry instead of as an angry reporter poised to take the system down? Had I really needed only a simple comment from Nick to point me in the right direction over dinner? As it turned out, I was as capable of missing the obvious as the rest of them.

I spent the next two hours sailing through case reports on drugs, reading the never-ending fine print of possible side effects (surprise! one was missing), and scouring the profiles of Dexter-White executives. Typing in "Dexter + White + invisible" led me nowhere. Invisible women around the country were out there working alone in the dark. How had we failed to coalesce into a movement? How had no one taken us seriously? Maybe because we were timid and hurt, having already spent so many years feeling invisible before the truth of the matter kicked in. If we didn't have the starch to tell our own families that no one could see us, then how could we be ready to tell the world?

As I put together a list of questions I would ask the Dexter-White chemist if he would ever stop canceling on us, I started to yawn. It hadn't been a very good night's sleep. I'd spent most of the night staring at the ceiling, thinking about what I was going to write if Ed would only let me. But now I was on to a story that could be much bigger than our local paper, a story that had comeback written all over it. I was thinking like a reporter again, and to that end I needed some caffeine. I left the library, stopping to lock my computer in the trunk of the car, and walked down the block to a little coffeehouse called the French Press, where young people drank lattes and wrote poetry and tried to pick each other up. I was placing my order for a regular cup of coffee when I heard a brief, familiar laugh behind me. I turned around and saw my son sitting on a high stool hunched over his computer. Miller Kempton was beside him. Right or wrong, I made my decision almost instantly. Leaving my coffee, I went back to my car, stripped off my clothes, hid the keys on top of the back left tire, and headed back to the French Press.

After Nick graduated from Oberlin he taught American history to middle school students at a Chicago public school, but then the cutbacks came and the first hired were also the first to go. He sent out applications to just about every school that had an opening, private and public, Arizona to Maine, but he found himself in an ocean of well-qualified, unemployed teachers. Finally, he had to give up his apartment and leave Chicago. I knew Nick wanted to have his own life again, to get out of the house and find a job. I didn't see how my asking him too many questions would be helpful. But I was curious, and I was invisible. Sometimes I used my powers for the greater good of my fellow citizens, and other times I squandered them by snooping on my children. I was only human. I picked up my coffee, which had remained mercifully undisturbed in the spot where I left it, and put in a straw so I could lean over and sip just behind the boys.

"I still think we should go tonight," Miller said.

"That's because you want to get drunk first," Nick said. "I'm not doing this drunk and I'm not doing it in the dark."

Whatever it was, good for Nick.

"Here's a job," Miller said. "Dog grooming. We could groom dogs."

"Doesn't that require a little bit of skill?"

Miller shook his head. "We could practice on Red. We'll give flattops to all the poodles."

Nick tapped on the curser and rolled the screen down, looking for opportunities. "Maybe we should just resign ourselves to the army."

My heart froze in my chest.

"A fine idea, except that there's a war going on," Miller said.

"Right," Nick said. Then his hands came off the key-board and for a moment his nose went into the air. He turned behind him and looked right at me, then he scanned the room.

"What?" Miller said.

"I thought my mother was here." He shook his head, pushing the thought aside, but in another minute he got up and went to sniff the hair of a pretty girl who was sitting two stools away. She was reading an Italo Calvino novel and drinking a cappuccino. Her look was one of surprise but not complete displeasure.

"Is there something I can help you with?" she said.

Nick shook his head. "I'm sorry," he said. "I was distracted by your perfume."

"I'm not wearing perfume."

"Maybe I was distracted by your shampoo then." He stood up. "Then again I may be losing my mind."

"That's a shame," she said, and gave him a pleasant smile before going back to her book.

"I really do think I'm cracking up," Nick said when he came and sat down next to Miller.

"Some girl in here is definitely wearing your mom's perfume but I don't think that means we can just start sniffing all of them. Besides, 'You smell like my mother' isn't exactly the greatest pickup line I've ever heard. Now how about this for you," Miller pointed to the screen. "Legal secretary. I mean that would at least be a good warm-up for law school."

"Except I'm never going to get into law school because all the other unemployed history teachers in America have already applied and the ones that get in will someday become unemployed lawyers and those are the people who will fill out the five hundred applications to be a legal secretary."

Nick had applied to law school?

"Man, you are in a very negative place."

Nick hit Miller lightly on the arm. "Come on, let's get this thing done."

"Really?"

"Stone cold sober in the light of day."

Miller looked at his watch. "I'll be interested to see if the tattoo parlor has a lunch crowd."

"Are you out of—" I clapped my hand over my mouth. Nick stopped and looked again at the shampoo girl, who in turn looked at him and shook her head.

"This place is giving me the creeps," Nick said, and they were out the door.

Idiot boys! Needless to say, I stayed close as they loped down the street, looking so much like a couple of fresh-faced kids off to shoot hoops. When they opened the back door of the car to put in their computers and their back-packs, I jumped inside.

"Who told you about this place, anyway?" Nick asked.

His car was messy. There were soda bottles on the floor of the backseat, CDs without cases sliding around, a green hooded sweatshirt that belonged to his father rolled up in a ball, an empty sack from White Castle. I was getting ir-ritated about all of it.

"A guy I knew in high school used to work there. His tattoos were good."

"Did he get them there?"

Miller shrugged. "I don't know. This isn't the kind of thing where you can just check Angie's List. It's a tattoo parlor, I mean, I doubt they're rated."

They were both over twenty-one. Weren't they free to do what they wanted to do with their own bodies? No. The answer was certainly no. I had made one of those bodies myself and I wasn't about to let a temporary moment of stupidity mar it for the rest of its days on this earth. I was still the mother, after all. That counted for something.

"I swear to you I smell it again," Nick said.

Miller leaned back and sniffed. "Me too. It must be on you somewhere. Maybe your mom got some perfume on your wash or on your pack or something."

Nick thought about this for a minute. "I guess. That's the only thing that makes sense."

Miller sniffed again. "I've got to say it though, your mom smells fine."

"Drop it," Nick said.

We were heading for what Arthur referred to as the Down Side of Town. There were no railroad tracks, but if there had been we would now be on the other side. Pawnshops and check-cashing centers sat in the shadow of billboards that advertised the services of bail bondsmen. Miller was punching something up on his iPhone. "Thirty-three forty-three," he said, and with that Nick pulled into the Bleeding Heart Tattoo Parlor.

I was sitting in the back of the Honda Accord thinking about Nick's first day of kindergarten. After I had handed

him over to the teacher, all smiles, Nick waving goodbye
to me as if it were the most natural thing in the world, I
ran around to the back of the building, Evie on one hip,
and peered through the window to watch him. I was the
one who was crying. Nick was working the room like a tiny
politician, going to see what all the other kids were doing,
checking out their books and toys. He was so beautiful!
The most beautiful child in the room. He was blond in
those days, with big dark eyes; his ivory skin still unmarred,
not a single tattoo on that boy. He turned off the car and in
a split second I thought to grab his phone out of the side
of his pack just before he reached for it. The next thing I
knew they were walking inside. I have never punched out
numbers so fast in my life.

"Nick?" Gilda said, sounding surprised when she answered. "Everything okay?"

"It's me," I said. "And nothing is okay. I took Nick's phone.
Get a pencil. I'm at the Bleeding Heart Tattoo Parlor, 3343
Thompson Lane."

"How can an invisible person get a tattoo?" she said.
"That's insanity."

"Insanity, yes, but not my insanity. Nick and Miller are
in there now. I'm in the car but I'm getting ready to go in
and stall things until you can get here and bust it up."

"Miller's getting a tattoo!" Gilda said. "I'll kill him first.
Whose idea was this?"

"I have no idea. All I know is that it wasn't mine. I ran
into them at the coffee shop and was eavesdropping. When

they said what they were doing I followed them here. I mean I got into Nick's car."

"Oh, Clover," Gilda said. "Thank God you're invisible. Seriously, I don't know what we're going to do when you come back again."

Through the plate-glass window I could see the boys talking to a large, tattoo-covered man who looked like he had recently escaped from prison by way of the circus. "Listen, I've got to go," I said. "Just get here fast."

I got out of the car and tried to close the door quietly, then I stood outside the glass door of the shop looking in. It looked like a barber shop but with only two chairs. The interior was both plain and spare, a yellowed linoleum floor, a half wall of mirrors, pictures of possible tattoos secured with tacks—a flaming dagger, a twisting snake, an overwrought Celtic cross that looked like a pattern stamped out by a fancy waffle iron. It appeared that midday traffic was low, only the two boys and the tattoo man discussing the menu options. The tattoo man was wearing a gray sweatshirt with the sleeves cut off. One arm seemed to be where he or his brother tattooers had come to practice: two interlocking chain links, a very simple flag, a couple of names in script too elaborate to read, a bosomy girl balanced inside a martini glass. The other arm, however, was something of a masterpiece—a tree whose roots ran to his fingernails and whose trunk went up to his elbow, with a flourish of branches and leaves and a nest of birds on his upper arm, spreading into the darkness beneath his shirt. I saw the top

leaves climbing up the side of his neck. Maybe a few of the
birds had flown up into his beard. Impressive as it was, it
was not the kind of thing I wanted for my son.

There were no other customers in the parking lot who I
might have been able to slip in behind. People don't think
about the ways that being invisible can be tricky. If you don't
want to call attention to yourself it's better not to open a
door. Still, I wasn't going to stand on principle and watch
these children get inked. I went inside.

A bell jingled and all three of them turned their heads to
look at nothing. They shivered in the sudden burst of cold
air. "That's strange. That never happens." The big man almost walked right into me as he went over to open and close
the door himself. "Must be one hell of a wind." He shrugged
and came back. "So just the one word?" he said.

"That's it." Nick tapped his shoulder. "On the deltoid."

"How 'bout I put it in a bleeding heart? We've got a sale
on bleeding hearts now, buy one, get one free."

"That might be good," Miller said.

"Then get one on each arm," Nick said. "I just want
the word."

"Anything else on sale?" Miller asked.

"'Mother,'" the man said solemnly. "'Mother' is always
half price."

"How's that?" Miller asked.

"Because it's respectful," the man said. "People should
respect their mothers."

I had an awful lot to say on that subject but I managed
to keep my mouth shut.

"Look through the books," the man said, and pushed over two enormous books of the sort from which a person might chose a wedding invitation. "If you stick to just wanting one word, then you're going to have to pick your lettering."

Nick opened the book, glanced at two pages, and tapped on a row of type. "That's the one."

"You should be sure," the man said, looking down at his arbitrary choice. "These things last."

"It's fine."

Miller was perusing all his options. He was looking at a page of frogs wearing tiny crowns. But Nick was all business. Gilda might very well arrive in time to save her own son but she was going to be too late to save mine. Frantically I looked around for a distraction. I saw what appeared to be the workbench.

The big man turned the pages in Nick's book. "These are your color options."

"Black," Nick said without looking.

The man picked up Nick's wrist between his thumb and forefinger and turned it from side to side in the fluorescent light. "I'd suggest a dark navy. With your coloring the black is going to be too harsh. The letters just wind up looking like a bunch of bugs."

"You're the boss," Nick said. It was a stupid thing to say to a tattoo artist, but Nick was listless, as if he couldn't care less. Miller, on the other hand, was tapping on a little Aztec god. "This is pretty cool."

Nick looked over. "If you're an Aztec," he said. "But we're not Aztecs. We're unemployed."

There on the table was a boxful of small white paper packets. Using as much stealth as I possessed, I moved one to the table and silently tore it open. It was a needle sitting in a plastic bit with a clear plastic cap. How very sanitary of them. I had thought it would be a good idea to bend the needles but I could see now that it was a job that would take me most of the afternoon. Everything was so sterilized, so disposable. The ink was in tiny, individual pots. There were boxes of rubber gloves. I could throw the drill itself on the floor and step on it but I didn't imagine that that would go down well with the tattoo man and I still had my child's safety to think of. I kept looking out the window into the parking lot. Gilda, Gilda, Gilda.

"Take your shirt off," the big man said, and Nick obliged, unbuttoning his plaid flannel shirt and then pulling his T-shirt over his head. It was more than I could bear, seeing his slender white back in this cold room. I thought of those half-dressed boys sitting on Arthur's examining table, Arthur telling them to breathe in and breathe out as he listened with his stethoscope. Then the man handed Nick a piece of paper. "You better write it down," he said. "I never was great at spelling."

Nick printed out the word and handed the paper back to him. I leaned forward to look. *Unemployed,* it said.

"All right." I grabbed the paper and crushed it into a ball. "That's enough. Nick, Miller, the show's over. Put your clothes back on, get in the car, and go home." I had meant to be quiet, to wait for Gilda, but the words poured forth like marching soldiers that could not be stopped.

Nick stood up, as did the hairs on the back of his neck. "Mom?"

"That's right—Mom. You're finished. This is over."

All three of them were turning in slow circles, their chins pointed up to the humming strips of light. It was like a moment from *The Nutcracker*. It was the dance of the snowflakes.

"Your mom's here?" the tattoo man asked, scanning the empty room.

"Speakerphone?" Miller said, looking at the ceiling.

Nick patted down his pockets. "I don't have my phone," he whispered.

"Just go," I said. "And not to another tattoo parlor. You can forget about that, mister. I'll be there, too."

Suddenly Nicky's eyes welled with tears. "I've been smelling her all afternoon," he said in a low voice. "Miller, remember? We smelled her in the coffee shop and then in the car."

"Is your mother dead, man?" the tattoo guy said.

"Mom?" Nick said. "Are you—" He didn't say the word.

"I'm fine. No tattoos. That's it. Go, go, go." I held open the door and the two boys walked through.

"Right there," Miller said, stopping right in front of me. "I smell her there."

"Go!" I shouted in his ear, and then their speed increased. They were out the door and in the car and out of the parking lot in seconds flat.

The tattoo man came and stood beside me at the door. He gave his beard a scratch. "Just as well," he said, watching them go. "That was just about the most depressing tattoo anyone's ever asked me for, except the ones that are some dead guy's name. They didn't need it."

"Who needs it?" I said.

He shrugged. "Drunk boys, sailors, people who just fell in love, people who just lost their mother." He turned in my direction. "You're sure you're not dead?"

"Not the last time I checked."

"Well, that's good."

I saw Gilda pull into the parking lot doing about eighty-five. Her tires squealed as she spun toward the curb. "That's my ride," I said.

"I figured as much. You have a nice day," he said. He was very gallant for a man who had lost his only customers. He held open the door.

eleven

"I need you to take me back to my car," I said. "It's at the library."

"Are you going to tell me what happened?" Gilda said. It was clear she was trying not to scream.

"I blew it, that's what happened. I yelled at them. I told them to go. I was trying to wait for you to come and get them out of there but then Nick took off his shirt and the tattoo man was all but firing up the drill. I couldn't wait anymore."

"So they know you're invisible. Who cares? Sooner or later they were going to figure it out. All that matters is that you stopped them."

"You're right. I know you're right. It's just that now I wish I'd told him before. I wish I could have sat down at the kitchen table and told him like a nice mother would." Like Vlad's mother did, that's what I was thinking. It made me incredibly sad. "I shouldn't have sprung it on him."

"You should have sprung it on him if it kept him from getting a tattoo! You had to play your card, Clover. You didn't have any choice."

"Promise me you won't light into Miller about it, at least not until I've had the chance to talk to Nick."

"You mean you want me to go home and not kill him?"

"I think it's best for now. Nothing actually happened. He might not try to figure out what my role in all this was." I was not being particularly forthcoming. I didn't want Miller to know I was invisible because then Benny would know I was invisible, and if *Benny* knew it might be his invitation to start smoking pot again. Given the circumstances, I wasn't about to drop all of that on Gilda.

"What were they thinking about going to get tattoos in the first place, that's what I want to know. Were they drunk?"

"Not drunk," I said. "I think they were depressed. Or I think Nick was depressed. Miller may have been going along for the ride."

"What are they depressed about?" Gilda ran a stop sign. There was no one else at the intersection, but still.

I put my hand on her arm. "Listen, don't kill us, okay? That's not going to help anything." I was wearing my seat belt. Even I found the sight of a seat belt on my naked, invisible self to be slightly disquieting. "I think they're depressed about not having jobs."

"Is that what they said?"

"No."

"Then why do you think that?"

I sighed. I wanted to tell her they had decided to get the bleeding heart special with the word "Mother" written inside. "They were getting tattoos that said 'unemployed.'"

With that piece of news Gilda swung her car over to the side of the road. She took a deep breath and then dropped her head to the wheel. "I can't stand this," she said.

"I know," I said. "Neither can I."

It had been my intention to go home to face Nick, but once Gilda had dropped me off I didn't feel ready. I pulled on a shirt and a hat and drove over to Arthur's office instead. I decided the jig was up. It was time for me to pull him into his office and tell him everything. A very clear lesson had been presented to me today and for once I was going to act on what I'd learned. It's time for us to all come clean, I was going to say. I know you're sitting alone in your office at night looking at bikes and boats and planes, and Nicky is going to a tattoo parlor because he can't find a job, and Evie, well, Evie is a total mystery so let's skip her, and

I'm invisible. We have to start pulling together as a family instead of everybody dealing with their own problems individually. I need your help if I'm going to get through this, that's what I was going to say. I want us all to help one another.

Once I was in the parking garage I took my clothes off again and went upstairs. For some reason I figured that if I was going to tell Arthur I was invisible I might as well be completely full-frontal invisible when I did it. At the end of the hall I saw my husband rush by and I followed him. I meant to put my hand on his sleeve but there were too many people all over the place, nurses and children and mothers and drug reps and Lonnie who brought around the files. Arthur was moving quickly into a room and I slipped in behind him just before Mary closed the door. There was a mother in there waiting, a pretty girl with round blue eyes and heavy brown hair that hung straight down to her shoulders and was pushed back behind her ears. She was having her own bad day, and she was crying. Arthur took her baby from her arms and after a minute of stroking his head and saying how pretty he was, he put him down on a blanket on the table. He was maybe six months old. He cried a little but it was a tired cry and soon he stopped. Arthur listened to his heart and then touched his head again. He crouched down to look into the baby's ears. And when he bent forward I bent forward too and touched my forehead very lightly to his back. I breathed in the starch of his lab coat and let myself be comforted by the warmth he was putting out. I wasn't going to ask him for anything else. I wasn't going to ask him to finally notice what had happened to me, at least not now. This baby was sick. Even I could see that.

I opened the door. It didn't matter. People opened doors every ten seconds in that place. I went back to my car, got dressed, and went home.

I found Nick at the kitchen table. He was never one to hide. "Thin Man's pooch," he said when I walked in the door.

"Don't be ridiculous. You know that. Asta."

"I do know that," Nick said, filling in the letters, "but it's the one I was on."

For a second I thought I was off the hook, that he wasn't going to bring it up. Then he decided to continue.

"I've been able to come up with two options," he said, keeping his eyes on the crossword puzzle. "The first option, very disturbing, is that I am losing my mind. The thing that keeps me from being sure this is the case is that it would mean Miller is also losing his mind at the exact same moment in the exact same way, and this seems unlikely. I like Miller but we don't have that much in common. That brings me to option two, that somehow, in some way I cannot figure out, you're spying on me, following me around to coffee shops and tattoo parlors to find out what I do during the day. If that's the case, I ask you to not deny it, because if you deny it that leaves me with option one and that's not a great option."

Was it possible he still didn't know, didn't wonder, after all this? Granted I had dressed again in order to drive home but it really didn't amount to much of a disguise. "Okay," I said. "Option two. Do I get to defend myself?"

He glanced up, then he looked back at his puzzle. "No," he said. "I don't think you do."

"Well, I'm going to anyway. You told me I had to tell you the truth and now you have to listen to it." I threw my keys on the table and sat down. Red came barreling into the kitchen and leapt onto my lap, where he proceeded to lick my invisible face even though his breath smelled like fish. "I was not following you, not at first. I happened to go to the French Press for a cup of coffee. I didn't know you were there."

"I don't believe that. I'm always there."

"That may be, but at that moment I wasn't thinking about you. I was at the library and I was sleepy and I wanted a cup of coffee, that was it. But then I saw you and Miller and I heard you talking." I shook my head and started again. "Okay, I want you to imagine this: let's say you had never wanted a tattoo in your life but while you were out you overheard me and Gilda talking. You heard us say we were going out to get tattoos. Wouldn't you be a little worried? Wouldn't you maybe follow us to make sure we were okay?"

Nick closed his eyes. "I would not have been sneaking around trying to listen to your conversation in the first place."

"I wasn't sneaking. I mean not any more than I'm always sneaking. I was right there."

"I didn't see you."

"But you knew I was there because you smelled me."

And then Nick opened his eyes.

"I got into the backseat of your car and I went with you to the tattoo parlor. You saw the door open."

"Mom," he whispered, leaning forward. "Where's your head?"

Red barked twice and I scratched his ears. Nick watched the fur compress and then release beneath my fingers.

"You came into my room," he said. He was pale now. "You said, 'Can you see me?'"

"That was when it all started."

"That was," he stopped and swallowed. "That was a long time ago."

"I should have told you."

"How did it happen? Did you get electrocuted? Did something horrible spill on you?"

"It was nothing like that. I think it has to do with a pharmaceutical company called Dexter-White. I think I took the wrong combination of pills. I'm trying to figure that out."

"Does everybody know? Did you and Dad just decide not to tell me?"

"Oh, Nicky, no, nothing like that." I reached over and put my hand on his wrist and he stared at it like it was making him uncomfortable so I took it away. "Dad doesn't know, Evie doesn't know. I walk around all day and nobody knows. It's kind of a remarkable thing. Nobody gets it."

"Dad doesn't know?"

"I kept thinking he would figure it out, and now there never seems to be a good time to tell him."

"He thought you were depressed. He talked to me about it." Nick shook his head. "So who knows you're . . ." Either he couldn't find the word or he wouldn't say it.

"Gilda knows, and Grandma. They figured it out right away. I go to an invisible women's group at the Sheraton. I've made some friends there. Do you remember Mrs. Robinson, your second-grade teacher?"

"And here's to you, Mrs. Robinson?" Nick said, but he didn't sing it.

"She's in the group. She's invisible now."

Nick kept shaking his head back and forth like a slow pendulum and Red's head went back and forth as he watched him. "Anybody else?"

"What difference does it make?"

"Because I'm feeling like a complete jerk and I guess I'm wondering who isn't a jerk."

"It isn't like that. I think that people just don't look at one another anymore, or they look at girls like Evie or the shampoo girl whose hair you sniffed, but they don't look at anybody else. I don't want you to take this personally."

It was at that unfortunate moment our houseguest walked in the kitchen, mercifully without Evie, and assessed the scene in front of him, looking carefully at me and then at Nick. I made a face that said, Please, Vlad, keep your mouth shut. It did me no good.

"You told him," Vlad said.

I put my head down on the table.

"You told Vlad!" Nick said. "He's in the house for one night and he knows you're invisible?"

Vlad reached behind him and closed the door. "It's not what you're thinking."

In half a second Nick was on his feet, his chair shooting out behind him. "Why don't you tell me what I'm thinking, farm boy?"

Vlad, who, it turned out, was the star of the Ohio State hockey team, held up his hands. "I swear to you, I felt the exact same way."

And that was it. Nick took a swing at him, punching Vlad, who was a great deal taller and wider, in the side of the neck. The connection made a dull, smacking sound. Vlad used the other half of the second to lunge for Nick but then he thought better of it. He stood back and chose not to kill my son and for the second time I thought how lucky my daughter would be to marry such a man. Unfortunately Red jumped off my lap and bit Vlad then, tearing his jeans but, thankfully, not the skin.

"Red!" I shouted, and Red released. "His *mother* is invisible," I said, grabbing the back of Nick's shirt. "I didn't tell him. He figured it out."

Vlad was rubbing the side of his neck. "Fuck," he said, and then he said, "Excuse me."

"Go right ahead," I said.

"Oh, man," Nick said, his head still turning back and forth like it would never stop. "Man, I'm sorry."

"I wanted to punch somebody when I first found out,

but I didn't do it. Don't ever punch someone in the neck," he said.

"Does Evie know?" Nick said.

Vlad held up his hands. "I didn't tell her. I have no plans to tell anybody anything. Based on how this one went down I think it would be a good idea if everybody cooled it for the night. Let's just digest what we know." He looked at Nick. "If you're okay with that."

"I think we should—" Nick stopped. "Never mind. I don't know what I think."

Vlad opened the freezer and filled a dish towel with one enormous handful of ice cubes. "I'm going to let you two get back to your conversation. I'm going upstairs where it's safe."

"What are you going to tell Evie about your neck?" Nick asked.

"I'm going to tell her it's a hickey," he said, and went out the door.

After that Nick and I just sat there looking at each other. It was easier for me than for him. "This is very weird," he said.

"It is," I said. "Though not quite as weird as getting a tattoo that says 'unemployed.'"

"Seriously? Are we still even thinking of that?"

"I am. I've had a while to live with the other part."

Nick laughed. It was a much-needed addition to my afternoon. "Everything's perspective, right? This morning it seemed like a great idea to have the word *unemployed* carved into my shoulder. It meant I stood with the masses of the suffering. I was at one with the common man. Let's just say that now I'm not feeling quite so sorry for myself."

"Because you're feeling sorry for me?"

Nick gave me a solemn nod even though he was still smiling. "Yes. Now I'm feeling sorry for you."

"Well, if it means you're not getting a tattoo, I'll take it. So are you going to tell Evie and Dad? Are you going to tell Miller?"

"Who you tell is for you to decide. I'm not going to out my own mother, who, I would hope, has no plans to out me either. Dr. Dad doesn't need to know we all went to the tattoo parlor today."

"I'd agree with that."

Nick yawned. "I think we should both take Vlad's advice. I just want to cool it for a minute. This whole thing took a lot out of me."

I looked at the clock hanging over the kitchen sink. Somehow, amazingly, it was nearly four o'clock and I hadn't given a thought to dinner. And then I realized I hadn't given a thought to anything. "Nick, my article."

"What article?"

"That's why I was in the library today. I wrote an article for the paper about the robbery and I forgot to turn it in." I ran out to the car and got my computer. The case was freezing and I wondered just how cold a computer could be before all your work disappeared.

Jeanne Ray

"Did you have anything to do with the robbery?" Nick asked in a hesitant voice.

"I took the guy's guns, that was all."

"Oh, thank God," Nick said, and closed his eyes. "That's so much better than you trying to rob the bank."

A footnote to the afternoon: Ed thought the piece was terrific. The phone rang twelve minutes after I sent it in. He said I could have all nine hundred words. "Send me stuff like this," he said, "and I'll put you in the paper every day."

"There isn't going to be a bank robbery every day," I said. "At least I hope there isn't."

"But there's always going to be something," he said. "Trust me on that."

And I did.

When Arthur came home that night I thought things were a little stilted, what with Vlad and Nick trying not to look at each other and looking entirely too much at me, and Evie rattling on about cheerleading and how they needed to get back to school tomorrow for practice, and Arthur, in the dark on everything, talking about a mother who refused to have her baby inoculated against polio because she'd read somewhere online that polio had been eradicated. He shook his head. "People can be very, very stupid," he said to the children. "This is a quality I urge you to avoid in yourselves."

"I'm working on it," Nick said. "I've had some good guidance."

"I'll get the dishes," Vlad said, standing up and taking my plate.

Evie put down her fork. "That isn't fair," she said. "You had to do the dishes last night. Nobody should have to do the dishes two nights in a row."

"Mom does the dishes every night, you moron," Nick said to his sister. Vlad stopped and looked at Nick and in return Nick pressed his lips together and nodded his head. He got up from the table and began to fill his hands with plates. "Vlad and I will do the dishes."

"Then what am I supposed to do?" Evie said.

"You can do the pots," Nick said. "Come on. It's going to be some kind of crazy fun."

There on the fence between curious and petulant, our daughter finally rose from her chair and hesitantly gathered up the glasses so that she could follow the boys into the kitchen. "That was a first," Arthur said, the two of us suddenly alone at the table.

"That Vlad's a good influence," I said.

"Tell me something," Arthur said, absently looking back toward the door to the kitchen. "Do you think they'll ever leave?"

"Vlad just got here, and Evie hasn't been back any time at all."

Arthur shook his head. "That's not what I'm talking about. I mean, do you think they'll ever all leave at the same time?"

"Is this about Nick finding a job?"

Arthur tilted his head from side to side as if trying to fix on the true nature of his question. "Nick will find a job, but then Evie will graduate from college and she won't find a job. She'll move home and then she'll miss Vlad too much and so he'll move here too, and then Nick will lose his job and Evie will have a baby—"

"What in the world has gotten into you?"

"Don't get me wrong," my husband said. "We'll love this baby. Our first grandchild."

"Arthur, seriously, did something happen at work today?"

He sighed. "Sometimes I wish we had a little time alone."

I wished I could reach out and squeeze his hand. I thought of him in his office in front of his computer. I thought of the baby that was sick. I thought of how tired he must be some nights. "The children will grow up and move on and we will miss them terribly," I said in a voice once used for bedtime stories. "We'll look back on this conversation with disbelief thinking of how lucky we were to have them around." I didn't know if this was true but I hoped it would be true.

"Go on," he said.

"We'll miss them, but only when we have the time. We'll be very busy."

"Doing what?" Arthur was still looking at the door, as if willing them to stay in the kitchen.

"We're going to get an old river barge and fix it up ourselves, a big old wooden boat. Then we're going to take it up the Rhine." This very cleverly alleviated my problems with sailing and seasickness.

"How do we get it to the Rhine?" Arthur asked. He was smiling now.

"Don't ask a lot of questions. It spoils the story." I lowered my voice. "We keep two bicycles on the barge and in the afternoons we tie up the boat and we ride to the little villages and buy bread and wine and cheese and then we have picnics on grassy slopes." I had worked in the boat and the bikes but I felt that throwing in a plane might tip my hand.

"We'll write the children postcards and tell them how much we miss them," Arthur said. "We'll write to them from the grassy slopes."

"Exactly." I was whispering. "But for now I'm going to take this opportunity to call it an early night. It's felt like a very long day."

"Music to my ears," Arthur said, pushing back from the table. "If I don't go to bed right now I'm going to sleep on the dining room table."

But when we finally were in bed, the lights off and the door closed against children who were doing God only knew what downstairs, Arthur whispered to me in the darkness, "I had such a powerful feeling about you today. Feeling . . . that's not exactly the right word. Maybe it was a premonition, except it wasn't about something that was going to happen. It was just about you. It was like you were standing in the room with me."

"Hmm," I said, because I had no idea what else to say.

Arthur snuggled up behind me, kissed my neck. "It was a visitation. An extremely pleasant visitation. That's what it was."

"I'll try to come more often," I said, and then, because the door to the bedroom was locked and the children never dreamed that such things happened anyway, I rolled over, suddenly less sleepy than I'd been, and kissed him.

twelve

*T*here was a 7:30 meeting at the Sheraton on Tuesday
mornings. Usually I didn't go because it was too tricky to
explain where I was off to so early (and you had to get there
way before 7:30 if you wanted to get out of your clothes
and up to the Magnolia Room on time), but this morning I
really needed a meeting. Even if I was only going to sit and
listen, I needed to be in the room with invisible women. I
told Arthur his mother was having an early bird yoga class.

"Give Mom a kiss for me," he called out from the shower.

Irene would never mind being my alibi.

.   .   .

I was just rushing, darting into the locker room to take off my clothes, darting down the hall and just making it into the elevator before the doors shut. All I was thinking about was the time, making the meeting, not being late. I had gone two floors before I realized I was standing next to Gilda. She was wearing a blazer and a skirt, which was for Gilda extremely dressed up.

"Gilda?" I touched her shoulder and she jumped.

"Jesus, Clover, you've got to stop scaring me."

My heart was racing. She was looking for me, something was wrong. "What happened?"

"Nothing happened," she said. The elevator dinged, fourth floor, and the doors slid open. "I just felt like going to a meeting."

"What do you mean you felt like going to a meeting? You're not invisible."

"In a lot of ways I am," she said philosophically, taking the lead down the hall toward the Magnolia Room. "My children don't pay any attention to me. They're off getting tattoos. My husband is having an affair with his iPhone."

I took her arm and pulled her aside. "You can't come."

"Listen, Clover, you're not the only person around here who feels in need of a little group support. We're friends. We do things together. If this is good for you, then it's good for me, too. Why would you have a problem with that?"

"You know full well why I'd have a problem with it. If

you didn't think I'd have a problem, you would have asked me yesterday and we would have ridden over together. You wouldn't be sneaking up on me in the elevator."

"I was in the elevator first," Gilda said sharply, but then her face softened even though she was looking far over my left shoulder. "Be a pal. Let me come. I want to meet your invisible friends. I promise I won't embarrass you."

I looked at Gilda's watch. I had seen several Kleenex go past us already. "Okay," I said finally. "It's a really bad idea but okay. And next time promise me we'll talk about it first."

Gilda nodded her head with great solemnity. "Promise."

We walked in together. I held her hand and held my breath. The invisible women were a friendly bunch, I told myself. A dozen Kleenex turned in our direction. I cleared my throat. "Everybody," I said, trying to sound bright. "I brought a guest today. This is my friend Gilda."

There was nothing, not a flutter, not a wave. A floating coffee cup came to rest on the table.

"Come on, guys," I said, wanting to sound light instead of pleading. "She really wanted to come. She's my best friend. She's been incredibly supportive of me."

"She isn't invisible," Jo Ellen said flatly.

Gilda nodded her head. "I know that," she said.

"This is a meeting for—"

"Invisible women," Lila said, and her Kleenex went up in gentle greeting. "So what? If she's a friend of Clover's—"

"The entire world is for them," someone said, but

I couldn't figure out who it was. "Can't we have a single place—"

Gilda turned to me. I was still holding her hand. "This is more complicated than I thought."

"No it's not," Laura Worthington said, raising her Kleenex. "We were visible not that long ago and with any luck we'll be visible again. If I come back to my old self I don't want to think I'm going to be drummed out of the meetings."

"You could always be in the meetings," Jo Ellen said. "Once invisible, always—" She stopped herself.

We were all still standing there around the Danish table. "I'm sorry," I said, my heart breaking a little. "I think we should go."

"Vote!" Alice said, her voice loud and clear. "All in favor of Clover's friend Gilda being an honorary invisible woman, raise your Kleenex!"

It didn't happen all at once, but ultimately eleven Kleenex went up. Two stayed down.

"A landslide," Lila said. "Take a seat."

"Careful where you sit," I whispered. "Not on a Kleenex."

Gilda was pale. She was cutting off the circulation in my fingers. "I want to shoot myself." Her voice was very quiet.

"I know," Alice said to her. "But you'll get over it."

"Now that we've had our excitement for the day," Jo Ellen said, "does anyone have something they'd like to talk about?"

After an awkward pause, Roberta spoke up. "Hi, I'm Roberta, and I'm an invisible woman."

"Hi, Roberta!" we said. Gilda joined right in.

"I've been invisible for about seven months now and at first I have to say I was pretty depressed. I just stayed in the house all the time. I didn't feel like I could drive the car. I didn't want to go to the grocery store. I was fired from my job as a nurse, though really I don't know if it was because I was invisible or because I was crying all the time. I just felt so embarrassed, like everyone was staring at me and I couldn't explain what had happened because I still don't understand it myself."

"Speaking of which," Jo Ellen said. "What's the update on the meeting with the Dexter-White chemist?"

"Could you let her finish talking first?" someone said.

"It's okay," Roberta said. "It's sort of emblematic of what I'm talking about."

"He keeps changing the date," Rosemary said. "He says it's because he's busy but I think he's nervous."

"Well, just be sure to keep on him and give us the updates. Roberta, I'm sorry," Jo Ellen said. "You were saying."

Roberta began again. "My husband and my kids didn't notice I was missing. I'd ask them to pick stuff up for me at the store and they'd do it. I was home all the time and the house was really clean and the food was great and everything was washed and ironed and put away. I brushed the dog a lot. I think they knew that something was different but as far as they were concerned it was better. They were happy, so, you know, end of story."

"Are you kidding me?" Gilda said. She leaned in the direction of the voice. "That's horrible. I mean, I know

Clover's family didn't notice she was missing but I thought it was just them, they're busy, they're obtuse, whatever. Are you telling me this sort of willful insensitivity is endemic to the entire situation?"

"Pretty much," someone said.

Gilda shook her head. We could all see on her face the pain she felt for Roberta, for all of us, and seeing it felt good. Maybe we'd needed one regular woman at the meetings all along. It was so satisfying to have a visual to go along with the story. "Forgive me," Gilda said. "I've interrupted you, and I want to hear your story. What happened next?"

"I had so much time on my hands I started reading the entire paper, the business section, the sports section, the want ads."

"The want ads!" we all said together.

"And by the way, Clover, great piece about the bank robbery. We were all glad you were okay."

"Thank you," I said, feeling excited. I hadn't seen the paper before I left.

"She was great!" Gilda said in a stage whisper.

Roberta went on. "And that's how I found my way to this group. The first time I came I took the bus. I wore a wig and sunglasses that were so big they would have embarrassed Jackie Onassis. I can hardly believe I was ever that person. Now look at me—I'm talking, I'm naked, and all of it's thanks to you. The women in this room literally saved my life. And now, because of the great example set by Lila Robinson, I'm back on the job as a nurse. They don't know it yet but I'm there flushing out IV lines, rubbing people's feet. It reminds me of why I wanted to be a nurse in the first place. I wanted to help people, not make sure that I was meeting the requirements of the charge nurse. Of course I'd like to get paid again—"

"We'll get paid again," Lila said, and ran her Kleenex through the air.

"I think that's right," Roberta said. "So, thank you, everybody."

"Thanks, Roberta," we said.

Gilda took my Kleenex and wiped her eyes. "I can't believe you women. You're so brave. Why aren't you on *Oprah*?"

"We don't make good television," Laura Worthington said.

"Anybody else?" Jo Ellen asked.

A Kleenex went up right away. "It's Patty Sanchez."

"Hi, Patty."

"I wanted to tell you that I'm taking piano lessons. A couple of weeks ago I called a woman in our neighborhood who gives lessons in her house. My boys used to take from her when they were younger. I just called her up and said, hey, I want to take piano lessons and I'm invisible. Are you okay with that?"

"You just told her straight out?" Gilda said with an enormous smile. Gilda had the loveliest smile. "Good for you!"

"Why not? She was interested, you know, she had some questions about what had happened. She wanted to know if it was contagious."

"Are you serious?" I asked. "What did she think, it rubs off?"

"People are ill-informed," Patty said. "That's our fault. If invisible women had a higher profile—"

"If we were more visible," Alice said.

Everybody laughed. "Whatever," Patty said. "I'd rather that she just said what was on her mind instead of making up some excuse about why she couldn't give me lessons. And I'm telling you, the piano is great. I don't know if it's because I'm older or it's because I'm invisible but I feel no sense of embarrassment whatsoever. I come home and I practice for hours, I don't care what it sounds like. I mean, this is my chance. When else would I ever learn how to play the piano?"

There was a nice round of applause for Patty.

"Is that everybody?" Jo Ellen said. Jo Ellen was one to wrap things up on time.

My Kleenex shot up. "Hi, I'm Clover."

"Hi, Clover!"

"I'll make this quick but I wanted to tell you I overheard my son talking to his friend in a coffee shop yesterday. His friend is Gilda's son. It was a complete coincidence that I was there but they were talking about getting tattoos."

The group let out a moan, the collective heartbreak of all suburban mothers.

"So I got in the backseat of his car and I rode to the tattoo parlor with them and I busted it up. I sent them home."

How? How? How? Everyone wanted to know.

"She just went in there and told them to leave," Gilda said, the color rising in her cheeks at the memory. "She didn't care. She saw what needed to be done and she did it. This woman is brave, I'm telling you, she's a hero. All that stuff you read in the paper about the bank robbers throwing their guns away, they didn't throw their guns away. I was right there and she's the one who did it." She pointed in my general direction. "My friend Clover Hobart took them down."

And with that the invisible women commenced to holler and cheer and carry on to such an extent that finally a manager came and opened the door of the Magnolia Room and there he found nothing but Gilda and fourteen empty chairs arranged into an imperfect circle. "I got some good news," she said, holding up her cell phone to him, then she stood up and walked out of the room.

After the meeting, Gilda had an appointment to get her teeth cleaned, one more ritual of human upkeep in which I could no longer participate. I went home to find the boys in the kitchen, both of their laptops open, both of them pecking away. Vlad was wearing a homemade sweater with a homemade scarf, even though it was hardly that cold in the house. All he was missing to secure a role in *La Bohème* was a cap and a pair of fingerless gloves. I had a feeling he meant to protect us from the bruise on his neck. "Where's Evie?" I asked.

They both looked up at me and gave a very similar shake of their heads. I looked at the clock. It was just past nine. "So what are you doing up?"

"Do you know how many lawsuits Dexter-White has pending against them?"

"No idea," I said, pouring myself a cup of coffee. Good boys, they had made an entire pot.

"If we could get all the invisible women together," Nick said, looking at his screen, "we could have the class-action lawsuit of the century. Of course you'd have to wait until I was finished with law school so you could let me file it. How many of you are there anyway?"

"Again, no idea. Just remember, I'm not looking to get rich off this. I'd just like to be able to see my own hands again, and to keep it from happening to other women in the future."

"We've decided to divide up the research," Vlad said. "I'm looking into the medical aspects and Nick is taking the legal. I called my mom and she didn't know anything about Dexter-White, but I got a list of all the pills she's taking." He held up a piece of paper. I didn't need to read it.

"Premacore, Ostafoss, and Singsall," I said.

Vlad's mouth dropped open but he did not speak.

"Chances are she also had an injection of Botox at some point but she might not have mentioned that."

"You did Botox?" Nick said.

"Once," I said. "And keep your judgment to yourself."

"We've got to find someone in the company," Vlad

said, visibly shaken. "Somebody on the inside who'll talk to us."

"We've found him, or at least Rosemary found him. He's agreed to meet with us but he keeps getting cold feet, changing the date. We're sort of in a holding pattern."

"A *holding* pattern," Nick said. "Since when do you sit around waiting for your sources to call you back? I thought you were a reporter." He slid the paper across the table and there I was, below the fold but still, front page. "Nice article, by the way."

I picked up the paper. THE VIEW FROM THE FLOOR, by Clover Hobart. It felt pretty good.

"If you know somebody there I think we should go," Vlad said.

"We should go?"

"Sure," Nick said. "We're in this together."

I kissed my son on the top of the head and then for good measure kissed Vlad as well. "As much as I appreciate it, this is a job for invisible women. If this source is any good we don't want to scare him off. You be the lawyer, you be the medical researcher, and I'll be the reporter. That said, I want you to give me all the information you've got."

"My mom is just going to freak when she hears about this," Vlad said under his breath.

Called to action by the pressure of two boys, I dug through my yoga bag until I found the phone number of

Irene's former student Jane in New York. I told her who I was and explained the situation. "Any chance you're visible now?" I asked hopefully.

"I'm as clear as an autumn night," she said. "Who's the guy from Dexter who said he'd meet with you?"

"I think his name is Wilhelm something. He talked to Rosemary in our group."

"I don't know any Wilhelms, but I sure wouldn't sit around waiting for him to agree to meet with you at the Cheltenham Target. Come on up and I'll take you out there. If there's any opportunity with these people you have to go for it."

"Take us to Target?"

"Heavens, no. I'll take you to Dexter-White. The place is huge. E-mail me his last name and I'll figure out where his office is. The element of surprise is always our greatest asset. You're better off to just storm the castle, catch him off guard. Terrorizing the people at Dexter-White is starting to become my full-time job. Frankly, I could use a fresh perspective."

"When would be a good time for me to come?" I said. "I'll have to check with Rosemary too."

"Tomorrow," Jane said. "I was going out there anyway. Try to come in as early as possible. I can pick you up at the airport in Philadelphia."

"Tomorrow?"

"We should get moving on this," Jane said. "Any Dexter-White employee who is willing to talk to an invisible woman isn't somebody who's going to be around there for long. Let me know what time your flight comes in. I'll be waiting at baggage carousel three. I'll be the invisible woman wearing red pants."

After Jane had hung up I sat there holding the phone for a few minutes. I had been waiting to go to Philadelphia for weeks now and yet tomorrow felt entirely too soon. It was like finding out the test had been rescheduled and I hadn't been studying.

"Tomorrow?" Rosemary said when I called her.

"It wasn't my idea."

"Tomorrow isn't possible. I have work in the morning and then Katy has her big orthodontist appointment in the afternoon. It's a major tightening. She's been dreading it for weeks."

"Then she'd probably be thrilled if you put it off."

"These appointments are impossible to come by," she said. "And then tomorrow night we have Mark's parents' anniversary party. We haven't told them I'm invisible yet so I wouldn't have a good excuse about why I wasn't there."

I could make up good excuses for her all day long. "Which anniversary?" I asked.

"Fifty-second. Why does it matter?"

"Because you can skip the fifty-second anniversary, just not the fiftieth. Anyway, we'll probably be back in plenty of time for the party."

"I shouldn't risk it," Rosemary said.

I sighed. Who knows, maybe I was relieved. "Okay, I'll just tell her it's going to have to be another day. Tomorrow is very short notice. Look at your calendar and tell me—"

"No!" Rosemary said, a little too loud. "It has to be to-morrow. Jane's right. We've put this off too long as it is."

She was happy about it! Or at the very least she was relieved. "You want me to go alone? Rosemary, he's your contact. You're the one he's talked to." I was letting my mind get ahead of me. Go around airport security by myself? Get on the plane naked?

"I only talked to him one time. He doesn't care if it's me, and even if he did it's not as if he'd be able to tell us apart. And you'll have Jane with you. There will still be two of you going."

"Not on the plane."

"Are you afraid to fly?"

"Well, I wasn't the last time I did it, but the last time I had a ticket and a suitcase. Have you gone on a plane by yourself since you turned up missing?"

There was a long silence. "Look," she said finally. "Jo Ellen assigned me to the Dexter-White committee and then I turned out to be pretty much the only one on it. I'm a librarian. I have good research skills. I didn't lose my job because nobody cares whether or not librarians are invisible. But I'm not like you. I get nervous when I have to ask people questions. To tell you the truth, every time Wilhelm's put me off I've been thrilled. I keep telling him, Great! Thursday was no good for me either! Even if I could go with you it would probably be a mistake. I could just wind up taking the whole thing down."

That was how it came to be decided that I would go to

Philadelphia alone with no clothes, no ticket, no money, identification, or phone. Oddly enough, the part that worried me the most was the idea of not having a book. I had sat beside people who boarded planes with nothing to read and I couldn't imagine how they had made such a serious mistake.

"I'll e-mail you all my files," Rosemary said before we hung up. "That way you'll know everything I know."

I, in turn, forwarded all of those files to Nick and Vlad, who were putting together essential fact sheets that I would memorize this afternoon and then leave behind. I felt like a spy being stripped of her former identity. I was going out into the cold.

"Explain to me one more time why I'm not coming with you," Gilda said on the way to the airport.

"Well, for one thing you don't have a ticket."

"Neither do you."

"And for another thing, you're not invisible. What are you going to do, fly to Philadelphia to sit in the car all day?"

"If it would be helpful."

I loved Gilda with all my heart because she would do it and think it was a perfectly sensible way to spend her afternoon. Nick and Vlad had also volunteered but it was a 6:30 a.m. flight. I didn't tell them that. I left while they were sleeping.

"What are you going to do if you get into trouble?"

"I'm going to call you collect. You'll have your phone on all day and you'll answer any number." We had gone over this a million times last night.

"And what if you can't find a phone?"

"I'll steal somebody's cell phone." This we decided would be okay as long as I also put it back. "Could we stop talking about what could go wrong? Nothing's going to happen to me."

"Didn't you read *The Constant Gardener*? Pharmaceutical companies can be the most dangerous places in the world."

"They'd have to find me first," I said as she pulled into the "Departing Flights" lane in front of the airport. "This is it."

"I'll be right here at seven ten tonight unless I hear otherwise." Gilda leaned over and hugged me, even though she usually wouldn't get near me when I was naked. "Be safe," she said.

I had come to the airport an hour before my flight just the way we're always told to, but it turns out that an entire hour is only what's necessary for visible people. I knew that flying was a drag but it wasn't until I could step outside the vastly complicated and demeaning process of trying to board a plane that I could see how bad it was. These people were herded like sheep, snapped at, admonished, redirected, bossed around like a bunch of little sisters, and they took it all mindlessly for fear that standing up for oneself in the name of good manners and common decency would get them booted from the line. The lines! They were everywhere, and what was asked of the travelers was constantly changing. After they stood in line at the confusing kiosk to get a boarding pass, they trudged off to another line where they held up their ID and boarding pass to show they were fit to enter the line where their ID and boarding pass would actually be scrutinized. It was only then that they were made to unpack their bags, remove computers and liquids, take off their belts, empty their pockets, remember their boarding passes, remove their cardigans, put their shoes in a bin, and then wait with enduring patience until they were called to walk through a scanner that lit up the fillings in their teeth. After that someone patted them down. It was a horror to behold. I resolved on the spot that if I could ever be seen again I was giving up flying.

Me, I swam upstream, went down the hallway marked "No Entrance" through which the arriving passengers poured, sailed past the guard who watched only for the people who might be coming in the opposite direction. I went to the bookstore and read the covers of all the magazines. I had so much time! I found a twenty-dollar bill on the floor and ran to put it in the pocket of an Indian woman who was cleaning the bathrooms. I tickled a baby who was crying in her stroller while her mother chased down a pair of three-year-old twins. I picked up paper cups and put them in the trash bin. I tried to make myself useful.

Following the advice of my invisible sisters, I was the last person to board the plane, which, mercifully, did not appear to be full. I slipped in just as the flight attendant began to wrestle the door closed. There was an empty seat in first class, a seat I was just about to take, when the man next to it folded up his jacket and settled it there like a precious object. I wasn't above sitting on someone's jacket but it seemed possible there could be reading glasses or a phone or something else that could prove to be both breakable and uncomfortable. I headed back to coach.

I made a quick appraisal of the available seats and who was sitting beside them and what they were reading and whether or not they seemed likely to dump a large bag in my lap after takeoff. By process of elimination I took 7B. The woman in 7A was maybe a few years older than I was, nicely dressed in a pearl gray suit and a large, lavender scarf, and possessed the winning combination of the new Philip Roth novel and a copy of *Dwell,* either one of which I would have been happy to read over her shoulder. I didn't fasten my seat belt, but honestly if the plane went down I didn't think it would do me all that much good anyway. All in all I had to say the entire process of flying seemed much simpler than I had thought it would. Once we were airborne I considered making a quick trip to Paris while I was in a position to do it so easily. What a treat it would be to skip the passport line and the customs check! I hadn't been to Paris since my junior year of college. Still, Arthur and I had always said we'd go together.

My seatmate opened her copy of *Dwell* and I leaned to the side as much as good manners would allow. There was an article about bamboo bathtubs that I found both dazzling and ridiculous.

"Invisible?" the woman whispered.

I sat up straight.

"Maybe I'm crazy." Her voice was very quiet. "But I'm a pretty good judge."

"Yes you are," I said.

She nodded her head. "I thought so. It's funny, all the seats on the plane you could have chosen."

"I wanted to read that Roth novel," I said.

"This will be easier if we change seats." She stood up and raised the armrest and I slipped over by the window. She put the novel in my lap, not that I ever opened it. "There," she said. "Now it doesn't look so much like I'm a crazy person talking to an empty seat."

"How did you know?" I whispered.

"I used to be invisible myself," she said. "After a while you have a very clear sense of when you're in the presence of your own kind."

"You came back!" I said, my heart leaping in my chest. "I can't believe it. I don't think any of us have ever met—"

"We're so disorganized." The woman shook her head. "There needs to be some central clearinghouse of information. Invisible women need to get their act together."

"How did it happen? What did you have to do?"

She shrugged. "I wish I could tell you but the whole

thing is somewhat of a mystery. I did a lot of things all at once. I took advice from a lot of different people. I took a sabbatical from work and gave myself over to this. I told people I was trying to find myself and let them draw whatever conclusions they wanted. I spent three months in an ashram in India, I drank a lot of wheatgrass juice, I took high doses of vitamin D, I went to Duke and did the rice diet, I tried steroids. I was very serious about coming back."

"So is it over? Are you visible all the time now?"

For a moment she looked uncomfortable and I said I hoped my question wasn't too personal. She shook her head. "It isn't that," she said. "It's just that once you've been invisible you understand that it could come back anytime. You never have complete confidence in your own matter. I used to flicker in and out, and then every once in a while I'd do a slow fade. In the last six months I've been pretty stable, knock wood." She looked around her seat. No wood. "Of course, who knows what we do in our sleep or when we're not paying attention."

"Sure," I said.

"I wish I had made a more controlled study of coming back. I wish I had tried things one at a time so I had a better idea of what worked. For all I know it could have been the ashram but maybe that didn't kick in for several months after the fact. I was taking the vitamin D the whole time, my doctor suggested that. I also think there's a chance it's just different for all of us. I mean my way back isn't necessarily going to be your way back. The stewardess is coming. Are you going to want a drink?"

"No, thanks."

When the flight attendant came by the woman shook her head. "I lead a pretty careful existence now, no alcohol, no refined sugar, no meat. If I really understood what had brought me back I think I'd be less worried about it. If I knew what had made me invisible in the first place I'd be a lot less worried."

"Are you serious? You don't know?"

The woman shook her head. Her hair was short and silvered, very pretty. I wondered if she'd stopped dying it because she thought it might have been the dye. "You used to take three drugs all manufactured by Dexter-White." I gave her the list. "At some point you also used Botox at least once."

She gasped so loudly that the man across the aisle leaned over and asked her if she was all right. "A little asthma," she said, and coughed. "I have my inhaler."

"Are you saying that it's just our little invisible women's club at the Sheraton that's figured this out?" I whispered.

My seatmate was shaking a little and I reached over and rubbed some circles on her back. "Just try and breathe," I said. "Do you really have asthma?"

She shook her head. "Not unless I'm getting it right now."

"You're not still taking those drugs, are you?"

"Of course not," she said. "I'm here, aren't I? How did you figure this out?"

"It happened before I joined the group. Everyone fills out a questionnaire when they start, except they do it later online since we don't really have any means of dealing with papers at the Sheraton. There were questions about everything—shampoo, carpet cleaner, laundry detergent, proximity to power stations. The only consistent factor was the drugs. All of us took the exact same prescription drugs, the same dosage. This isn't exactly a national study. The group has only been meeting for two years and on a day of perfect attendance we probably have fifteen members."

"I live in Princeton," she said. "I never had a group. A couple of times I'd see somebody, or not see them, someone like you, and we'd talk, but invisible women are so hard to keep track of. Dexter-White is practically where I live."

"I know," I said. "I'm going there now. I'm meeting another invisible woman and we're going to see what we can find out. I have a contact there, a chemist. I'm Clover Hobart, by the way."

"Erica Schultz." She held out her hand and I took it. "Let me give you my card."

"No purse," I said, "but I'll write down all my information for you."

When the plane landed Erica came with me to baggage carousel three to meet Jane, who was easy to spot in her red pants. It's pretty remarkable when you come up on an invisible woman wearing clothes. It seems almost impossible to believe she gets away with it without people screaming and pointing and running in terror but she does. Jane was thrilled to meet Erica and they exchanged information as well while the three of us stood around and talked, then Jane and I both hugged Erica goodbye and we stood there and watched her walk away.

"It's like meeting someone who escaped from Pompeii," Jane said.

thirteen

"I'd go to an ashram," Jane said to me in the car. "And I'd definitely take vitamin D and eat rice. I'm not entirely sure about the wheatgrass though. It's like drinking a glass of your front lawn."

"Irene drinks wheatgrass," I said.

"Well, see, there you have it. Irene's the toughest person I know. She was certainly the best yoga teacher I ever had. She could do anything."

"Sometimes I worry," I said, but I didn't finish my sentence. I was holding up my arm, looking through my hand at the other cars on the interstate.

"What?"

"Sometimes I worry that I like being invisible." I waggled my fingers. Nothing. "I mean, there are parts of it that are awful and I really do need to tell my husband, but before it happened I felt like I had all of the burdens of no one paying attention to me and none of the benefits. Now I can see how many things you can do when no one is watching. It's a huge freedom when you think about it."

"Well, it's your freedom and you're welcome to it," Jane said. "I for one want to look in the mirror and see something."

"Sure, I understand that, but for maybe the first time since I was fourteen I don't care what I weigh. I don't care how my clothes look because most of the time I'm not wearing any. I don't care that I'm getting older. I don't feel bad about my neck. I feel like a source of good in the world. Everywhere I go I'm making things happen. My life hasn't been like that in a long time."

"With all due respect," Jane said, "I would urge you to file those feelings away because we are now pulling into the parking lot of Dexter-White. If they've got a pill to reverse the process, then you can choose not to take it."

"Then again, I may just be steeling myself against disappointment."

"If things don't work out I'm going to call you every morning and ask you to repeat the whole speech to me. If I have to be invisible forever I'd like to be able to put a good spin on it." Jane turned off the car and started to take off her clothes.

I looked around. There was a sign right above us giving stern instructions as to who could and could not park here. "Um, do you think it's okay to park in the employees' lot?"

"Sure," Jane said, getting out of the car. "They never check."

The entrance to Dexter-White was through a security building that, while on a much smaller scale, was every bit as draconian as the airport. The few people in front of us were walking through a metal detector and having their briefcases searched. Visitors turned over their driver's licenses and filled out copious forms regarding the nature of their appointment while the people they were meeting were called to come down and claim them. We sailed through without documentation.

"What are they making in here, uranium?"

"The security is the first clue as to what's going on," Jane said. "These people have secrets and they have enemies. If we were visible women with a drug-based complaint we couldn't get past the first scanner. The public never makes it into this place. When I first found out Dexter-White was making us invisible I started calling them, trying to get an appointment to have someone sit down and talk to me. I couldn't even get anyone to return my calls. Then one day I thought, just go, they aren't going to be able to stop you."

"Have you talked to anyone?"

"Lots of people. They can be very polite when you're in

the room but they never do anything. They figure I'm invisible so I won't be able to bring them down."

As we walked through the campus of Dexter-White it reminded me of a movie set, a fake town that contained office buildings and houses and factories. People rode down the wide sidewalks in golf carts or walked in groups. They looked happy enough, and they looked smart.

"It's not the evil empire," Jane said, "not exactly. They're making a lot of good drugs, things people need. The problem is they're making too much money. If they were willing to suspend just one of the drugs, say the Ostafoss or the Singsall, just until they got the interaction problem worked out, that would be enough. But that would mean admitting that something was wrong, which would mean lawsuits and who knows how many countless millions or even billions of dollars they'd have to spend to straighten things out. They won't even run an ad saying not to take the medications together for fear of pointing out that they've known all along. Right now they're finding that sticking their collective heads in the sand is the most cost-effective means of solving the problem."

The longer we walked the more I realized that people were taking golf carts because the place was so big. It would be impossible to walk from building to building, back and forth, all day if you worked here. "How did you ever figure this place out?"

"It took a lot of time," Jane said. "Especially since I couldn't exactly ask for directions. I came back so many times that finally my husband and I decided just to move to New York so I could be closer. I didn't love all the flying anyway. It's okay when you get a seat but a lot of times you don't. I was always winding up with a rug burn. Our kids have all moved away, and my husband works as a consultant so he could be just about anywhere. We talked about living in Philadelphia but it wasn't right for us. I think I didn't want to be too close to this place. Sometimes I wonder what those smokestacks are blowing into the air."

I looked up at a set of smokestacks we were passing but for the moment they appeared to be empty and cold. "What did you do, you know, before all this happened?"

"I'm a painter."

"Oh," I said, "that's good. At least that's not a job you'd have to give up." I noticed the buildings were getting taller. I wondered if we were nearing the center of the Dexter-White universe.

"But the weird thing is I *have* given it up. I'm so distracted by all of this. All I want to paint are invisible women and that doesn't work. My art is pretty realistic."

"It would work," I said, because I could see these paintings very clearly in my mind as she was talking. "You could paint family portraits where the woman wasn't there. Or you could paint pictures of us just before it happened. The more I think about it, the more I see we were invisible then, too."

Jane was quiet for a long time and suddenly I was worried that one of us had wandered off. It was of vital importance that we not get separated. "Jane?"

"I'm sorry," she said. "I was just thinking about what you were saying. It's good advice, actually. You remind me so much of Irene. People must tell you that all the time."

"No," I said. "They don't, but it's nice to hear."

"Well, tell your husband he found a girl like his mother. What about you?" she said. "What did you used to do?"

It was an overcast day, no rain but plenty of bluster. The bare little trees stood in neat rows, not a single leaf on the ground. "I was a reporter, but that was a while ago."

"A reporter!" she said. "My God, no wonder you like being invisible."

We went through the double doors of a large building where yet another security guard was checking the badges of people who had had to obtain ten different levels of clearance in order to make it into this building in the first place.

"Leave nothing to chance," I said to the guard as we walked past and he nodded his head, never wondering who might have spoken.

"Wilhelm Holt is on the fifth floor," Jane said. "It's a keyed floor so we'll need to wait for just a minute until someone else is going up."

It did turn out to be just a minute because two men in gray suits came down the hall and punched the button, the elevator operators of our dreams. The four us went in together, and one of the men held his key card to the sensor and punched the sixth floor.

"Five, please," Jane said.

And without missing a beat he held his key up again and punched five. "Tony, I've got to say it, you smell good."

"Thanks," the second man said, giving a small smile in the direction of his shoes.

The door opened on five and we got out.

"What in the *world* was that about?" I asked.

"One day I was on the elevator for forty-five minutes trying to get to a keyed floor and no one was punching the right button. I don't mind elevators but I was about to go out of my mind, so finally I just said it, asked for what I wanted, and no one blinked an eye. Nobody looks at anybody in an elevator. And just for the record, it isn't Tony who smells good, it's you," Jane said.

We went down the hallway and when we were standing in front of Wilhelm Holt's door I asked Jane if we had a plan.

"Not exactly," she said in a quiet voice. "At least he knows that invisible women exist, so he's less likely to completely freak out. We'll just ask some questions, see if we can figure out what he knows. Let's try not to scare him."

We turned the knob and, very slowly, opened the door.

Wilhelm Holt was a small man whose bald head was fringed in a half circle of gray curls. He was wearing wire-rimmed glasses and a white lab coat, which made me feel fondly toward him in a Pavlovian way. His office was not particularly large, there was a desk with one chair behind it and two chairs in front of it, a bookcase full of books, a smattering of framed diplomas nailed to the wall. He was working hard on something, and while he was extremely focused he was also vaguely aware that the door was now closing and someone was in the room. "You should knock," he said.

"We should," Jane said, "but we didn't want to draw attention to ourselves."

He put down his pen and looked up, and when he didn't see anyone there he went back to his work without a single question to the air.

"Dr. Holt?"

"Yes?" he said, still working.

"My name is Clover and this is Jane. We're from the invisible women's group in Ohio. You spoke to my friend Rosemary on the phone. You've e-mailed her as well. You made plans to meet her at a Target store in Cheltenham, I believe in the shampoo aisle."

I had his attention now. His head was up and he was looking around the room as if he believed he could find us if only he tried a little harder. "You shouldn't have come here," he said. He was pale, but still, he had a world more color than either of us.

"I'm sure you're right," I said. "But you've already broken your engagement several times and, frankly, we got tired of waiting."

"How did you get in?"

"We're invisible," Jane said. "Figure it out."

"I was interested in helping you, or helping your friend Rosemary."

"Terrific," I said. "We're interested in being helped. And

don't worry about Rosemary. Her daughter had an orthodontist appointment and she couldn't get away. But invisible women are very interchangeable. You help one of us,
you help all of us."

He screwed the cap back on his pen and sat for a moment. "I don't like to be ambushed," he said. "I'm not pre-
pared for this."

"Take your time," Jane said. "We can wait."

"It isn't my fault that you're invisible," Dr. Holt said.
Now the color was coming back to his cheeks. Our visit was
inconvenient. He was getting upset with us.

"It isn't your fault," I said calmly, "but it is your responsibility. You work for a company that manufactures three
drugs that, when taken in combination, render women invisible, and despite our letters and phone calls and visits, no
one is doing anything about it. We need to see those drugs
taken off the market in order to protect other women, and
we need someone, possibly you, to figure out how to get us
back."

"No one is taking Singsall off the market. It's America's
most-prescribed antidepressant."

"I've found being invisible very depressing," Jane said.
"But I don't think I should take it anymore after what it's
done to me. You understand. Clover here is better adjusted
than I am. She probably has the energy to follow you home
and sit on your bed at night. We can do that, you know.
We're like lice, like bedbugs. Once you get invisible women
in your life it's almost impossible to get rid of them."

"Are you threatening me?"

"Yes and no," Jane said. "Really, I'm just being honest with you. Do I want to haunt you? No. I'm not a ghost. Will I haunt you if you make it absolutely necessary? Yes, I will, because even though I can see my children and my husband, I'd like for them to be able to see me. Something has to be done about this. This company has inflicted bodily harm on us and now they're ignoring the damages."

"So why me?" he said, his voice full of disbelief. "Why are you coming after me?"

"Well, in truth, it was because you were nice enough to take Rosemary's call," Jane continued. "No good deed goes unpunished, Dr. Holt. By talking to her you at least proved you know what's going on. You've heard about invisible women and you know their fate as it is connected to Dexter-White. That saves us from having to shake down every chemist and doctor and researcher in this place who spends his days torturing mice and would have no idea what we're talking about. Now if you want to turn over a list of your superiors, the people who you know are ruining our lives, we would be perfectly happy to bring our plague of locusts down on them, but you have to understand, we're coming down on somebody in this place and it's going to happen soon."

"I'm going to call security," he said, picking up the phone. "This is harassment."

"You shouldn't bother them," Jane said. "Even in a room this small we are impossible to find."

"Are you married, Dr. Holt?" I asked. There were pictures of him with his arm around a woman who was a head taller then he was. Neither one of them was particularly attractive. They looked happy.

"My personal life doesn't figure into this," he said.

"Oh, you might as well tell us. It's so easy to get into the backseat of your car and follow you home." I picked up the picture and held it out to him. "This woman here," I began. "Let's just say for the sake of argument that she's your wife. Let's say she's been through menopause and she's being eaten alive by hot flashes so her doctor gives her some Premacore. After that the same doctor finds that her bone density isn't quite what it should be and so he gives her some Ostafoss as well. But on top of that she's a little depressed. Can you blame her? She's just been through menopause, and you're working all the time, so he gives her some Singsall, just a touch, just to brighten up the picture."

"Clover, you're telling my story here," Jane said.

"All of these improvements come to your wife through the wonders of modern pharmacology. She didn't pick this combination out for herself, it's given to her. Then one morning you wake up and you've got nothing in your arms but a nightgown. Is that okay with you, Dr. Holt? Don't you think your wife deserves some help? Or do you figure now that no one can see her she doesn't have any rights? Would you sweep her under the rug, tell her not to make a fuss? She's been poisoned, Dr. Holt, by your company. She's been robbed of her very being. Are you going to tell her to go away?" I handed him the picture and he took it. He sat with it for a long time.

"We're working on it," he said finally. "We're not unaware."

"What are you working on?" Jane said.

"An antidote." Dr. Holt sighs and props the picture back up on his desk.

"I thank you. I'd love one. But that isn't good enough," Jane said. "At least one of these drugs has to come off the market. You can't make endless numbers of women invisible and then bring them back because it's better business. This can't be good for us."

"But it isn't endless numbers of women. In the control groups, only a very limited number of women became invisible."

"What?" I said.

"They knew this at the outset?" Jane said.

"If every woman who took these three drugs in combination became invisible, we would be losing people out of every city, every neighborhood. These are very popular drugs; some people would go so far as to say they are critically necessary. There isn't an outcry against this because not enough of you are gone. If you want a public outcry, try getting rid of Singsall."

"Good Lord," I said. I sat down in a chair at his desk. "If there isn't an outcry, it's because nobody else has figured out that you're the ones who've done it."

"Would you let your wife take these drugs together?" Jane asked.

Dr. Holt removed his glasses, rubbed his tired eyes. "Of course not."

"So where do you suggest we go with this now? Are you going to take us upstairs, introduce us to your boss?"

"Do you know how many years it takes to get a drug through development? We're going to need time."

"It doesn't take any time at all to pull something off the shelves. We're willing to settle for that for starters."

"I'm going to need more time," he said. "Let me push them. If I take you upstairs, the only thing that's going to happen is that I'm going to get fired, and all that means to you is that you've lost the one person who's sympathetic to your case. And believe me, ladies, I am sympathetic."

"And the rest of them aren't?" Jane asked.

"This is a business," he said. "A giant, multinational business. Whether or not you can see yourselves in the mirror is not of primary concern. I want to be in touch with you both. Actually, you could be invaluable in our studies. We've got drugs in development now but we're going to need invisible women who are willing to be part of the program."

"You want us to be guinea pigs?" Jane asked.

"You want us to take another Dexter-White drug? Why? So we can risk losing something else? Our speech? Our sight?" My hands were shaking. I had to restrain myself from turning over his desk, which, I believed, I was capable of doing.

"We would never put you in danger," he said. His voice was oddly soothing.

"Too late. You have forty-eight hours," I said. "Tell who-ever you want. You have exactly forty-eight hours to fix this and after that we're coming back."

"Forty-eight hours isn't enough time to change any-thing," he said. "It's not enough time to schedule a meeting in this place."

"But it's enough time for me to figure out what I'm going to do to you and everyone you work with if I don't see some action." I wanted to bite him. I wanted to kick. These were feelings unknown to me since junior high.

The door swung open and I had to assume Jane walked through it. I followed her out and down the hall, all but blinded by rage. They knew! They knew! The elevator doors were open and I got in. They don't make you have a key to get off the floor, only to get on. I stormed through the lobby, past the security guard and out the double doors, just barely able to contain myself until I was outside.

"They knew!" I said, my voice too loud. I was crying now, thinking of all the women who had been hurt and how little it had mattered to anyone. "We're nothing to them. We're a reasonable loss. We're a margin of error. It's one thing to be invisible but it's another thing to know that somebody did it to you and it didn't even matter to them because the prof-its were too high." I let out a huge breath, shook my head. "Come on," I said. "I just want to get out of here."

Nothing. In the distance there were some people walk-ing up the hill. I was by now standing in a grassy patch maybe twenty feet from the front door. It was like Singapore, everything was so neat. There wasn't so much as a gum wrapper blowing down the street. "Jane?"

Nothing.

Invisible women should not lose one another. This was imperative. Once separated we were as helpless as a pair of blind kittens. "Jane?" I said, and then I raised my voice. "Jane? Jane? Jane?"

Had I come out the right door? I went back into the building. The security guard lifted his head and watched as the door opened and closed and no one was there. On the other side of the lobby there was another security guard at another desk, another set of glass doors facing another grassy patch of lawn, another row of straight, leafless trees. I went and stood in the middle of the lobby, equidistant from the two men. There were enormous abstract paintings on the walls, a Calderesque mobile, or maybe even a Calder mobile, hanging down from the high ceiling, all no doubt holdovers from the eighties when large corporations bought large pieces of art. I tilted back my head. "Jane?" Both of the guards looked behind them. I exited the building in the other direction. "Jane? Jane?" I said into the wind.

I could remember I once lost Evie in the dress section of a department store. At first I thought she was playing. She liked to crawl between the clothes and hide in the bottom of the racks. I began to part them one at a time, looking down through the folds of fabric and calling her name—"Evie?"— but every time I looked my voice got a little higher, my heart beat a little faster. I couldn't find her. That was the last time

I felt this way—what I remember feeling that day was that I was lost, that I would be forever lost without her. Someone had picked up my child while I was looking for something to wear to a dinner party. I grabbed a saleswoman. I was already in tears. It wasn't two minutes before there was a voice on the loudspeaker calling out Evie's name. The entire store was quiet. And then a young woman in a black suit came up the escalator holding my daughter. Somehow Evie had gone down by herself and had not been able to figure out how to go back up. Crying and confused, she had wandered over to the Chanel counter, my Evie, four years old and drawn to the sight of lipsticks. The Chanel woman brought her back to me.

"Jane!" I called.

I began to walk in a slow, clockwise circle around the perimeter of the building, chanting her name like a prayer. I was thinking how odd it was that I had no idea what Jane looked like. I was thinking that if we ever got this worked out and if I ever got home again, I would have a party at our house and ask all the invisible women to wear their favorite outfits and bring pictures of themselves so that when I closed my eyes I would be able to picture them in my mind. What if somehow they had trapped her upstairs? What if Dr. Holt had a button under his desk that called security? They could have thrown a sheet over her or caught her in a net. In my mind I had terrible images of poor invisible Jane struggling against her captors. I went back into the building, much to the consternation of the guards. I decided to go back to the fifth floor, back to Dr. Holt's office. I would find out what they had done with her. I was waiting for someone to come and get on the elevator. I was wishing that Gilda was waiting in the car the way she'd wanted to, or Nick or Vlad. I wished that there was someone there to save us.

And then, as I pictured Gilda and Nick and Vlad all crunched together in the backseat, I remembered what I always told the children when they were younger: "Go to the car." I made everybody make note of where the car was every time we got out of it. I told them if they were ever horribly, hopelessly lost they should go to the car and wait there, and so I turned and made my way out of the building.

I didn't know what time it was. I missed wearing watches. The sky looked like dusk but I didn't know if it was bad weather or if it was really so late. I started to run. Every few minutes I called out again, "Jane!" I was almost to the parking lot when I saw the red pants and white top coming in my general direction.

"Clover!" she called.

"Jane!" I was bounding toward her.

"Clover!"

I threw myself in her arms. Not since I found Evie had I ever been so glad to see anyone, even someone I couldn't see.

"I came back to the car," she said, breathlessly. "I thought if I had some clothes on you might be able to find me."

"What happened?"

"He called me back in. I opened the door and then he

said he needed to know how to get in touch with us. You must have gone straight down the hall. By the time I got downstairs you'd already gone." She was holding on to my arm. We held on to each other all the way back to the car.

"Do you want to come back to the city and spend the night with us?" Jane asked. "My husband would love to meet you. It just seems like too much for you to fly back after all of this. We could talk some more, maybe come up with some ideas."

"I need to get home," I said. "My husband doesn't even know I'm gone."

And so Jane drove me back to the airport. We were too tired to talk anyway. "I'll call you tomorrow," I said. "I'll be back in a couple of days."

"We're a good team," she said.

We said our goodbyes and I headed in. It was late and the lines through security were long. If I'd had to stand in them, I would have missed my flight. There wasn't a seat going back, and so for a while I crouched on the floor near the bathroom, but then too many people needed to use the bathroom. I sat in the middle of the aisle but the flight attendants were bent on pushing their carts around, distributing cups of soda. I spent the entire flight squeezing into various small spaces, trying to avoid being stepped on. I would have hoisted myself up into the overhead bin and waited there but everyone brought carry-on luggage and there was not an available inch of space. It was a miserable trip and I felt extremely sorry for myself, thinking how nice it would be to

fourteen

Dear Gilda, pal that she was, was there to take me home. I gave her the overview but I was too demoralized to get into the details.

"But what happens next?" she asked as she pulled up in front of my house.

"I don't know," I said. "I haven't figured it out. But think about it, okay? Something's bound to occur to one of us."

Gilda leaned over me, squinted. "Is there somebody on your front porch?"

I looked out into the darkness. "I don't see anything." But then I did see something, a tiny point of orange light that for an instant got brighter and then faded.

"There!" Gilda said, pointing. "It looks like somebody's smoking a cigarette."

"Then it must be a friend of Nick's."

"I'll wait here," she said. "Unless you want me to go with you."

"I want you to go home. I'll be fine. If I can stop bank robbers I can certainly stop someone from smoking."

Gilda allowed that this was probably the case and so we said our good-nights. It was very dark. I'm the one who turns on the porch lights every night, turns on the lights in the living room. It appeared that there was no one home, unless you counted the person sitting on the front steps smoking. Maybe I could see some shoes, maybe a jacket. I really couldn't make out anything clearly. Some other night it would have been alarming, but tonight it was only one more thing to be added to the list.

"Hello?" I called out quietly.

The cigarette stood up. "You are Mrs. Hobart," a voice said. It was more of a pronouncement than a question. There was some accent, something I couldn't place. The orange light had one final, powerful glow, and then it fell to the ground and was crushed out by the shoe.

"I am."

"I am Ariana Sawyer, mother to Vlad. My son tells me you are invisible woman."

"Oh, Mrs. Sawyer," I said. "I'm so sorry I wasn't here to meet you. I've been in Philadelphia. Vlad didn't tell me you were coming."

"I did not tell Vlad. I tell Vlad, he would say Mother, stay home, do not make trouble for these nice people. But forgive me, Mrs. Hobart, I must make trouble for you. I can no longer bear to be only invisible person in the world that I know."

I reached out and took her hand. My eyes were adjusting to the darkness and I could see now that she was fully dressed, wearing tights beneath her skirt, wearing a hat. "I'm glad you came. Let's go in the back. The door is unlocked." As we went past the garage the motion light came on and Mrs. Sawyer stopped to look at me.

"You are very invisible," she said. "More so than me. Everything is invisible."

"I'm naked," I said. "I was traveling."

She took her hand from mine. "This is confusing."

"It's a long story. I had to fly and you can't fly unless you can show identification and I no longer resemble my identification."

"Naked," she said in wonder. Mrs. Sawyer was carrying a suitcase and I took it from her as we went inside.

"My husband must be working late." I looked around. Red came shooting out of the darkness and barked a stern reprimand. I gave him a biscuit. "I don't know where everyone else is."

"That is very cute dog." Red turned to her and wagged.

"Vlad and Evie have gone back to school. I called him when I arrived and he was horrified. He said I must drive home immediately. I said not until I have seen another invisible person. I could drive home now, Mrs. Hobart, if you are very tired, but to say the truth I would like very much to speak with you first."

"How far away do you live?" I asked.

"In Cookville. It is four hours away."

"Then you'll have to spend the night," I said. True, it wasn't the perfect night for a houseguest, but I had one and I would proceed accordingly.

"Thank you very much," she said. "May I trouble you also for red wine? I am sorry to ask but my nerves, they are not perfect. I have started smoking again. I smoked when I was a girl in Russia, never in the United States, never until now."

"Oh," I said, "Russia."

"Being invisible has been very trying. I have considered divorcing my husband. I have considered many things. My children tell me I am not in right mind but I do not say that to alarm you. You know the mind of the invisible person. It is what it is."

I found the corkscrew and the wine. I poured us each a glass. We toasted. "Very true," I said.

"Vlad tells me you went to Dexter-White to confront them about what they have done. Vlad says you are very brave woman."

"It isn't as hard being brave when no one can see you."

"I have found this to be the same. Did you get the company to agree to change us?"

"I think they'd like to change us but they don't know how yet. They lack a sense of urgency about the whole thing."

"That is because people cannot see. What you cannot see you do not care about. My husband proved this to me. Two weeks I am missing and he did not notice."

"I've got you beat on that one," I said, and took a long sip of wine. "And there are women in my group who have me beat as well. You should come to the meeting tomorrow. It's an entire roomful of invisible women."

"You are very understanding woman, very compassionate to husband. That is not the Russian way."

"Is your husband Russian?"

"My husband is thoughtless farmer whose people have been in Ohio since beginning of time."

"Then how did you meet?"

"I place ad in magazine and he orders me. This was 1982. There was then a big business in Russian brides. We all thought we would go to New York City, marry millionaire who gave us champagne in bed of silk sheets. That was not so. Still, it was a better life than the one I had before. I knew how to work. We were not unhappy until I disappeared. You come to a country and learn a man's language. He did not learn Russian, not single word, not hello or goodbye. I bore him three children. I fix his dinner and clean his house and feed his chickens. I make him sweaters. I work as secretary at State Farm insurance and I put all of paychecks into joint account. Everything I do, I do for him and when I was gone he did not notice."

"It's hard," I said. "But I tell myself it's because he knows me so well. He sees me even when I'm not there."

"That is very beautiful thought, Mrs. Hobart, but I do not believe it is true."

"Please, call me Clover."

"Ariana." Ariana tilted back her wineglass until it was empty and then placed it down on the table with a decisive click. "So, Clover, our husbands are not interesting. We must turn our mind to the cause."

"Dexter-White claims to be working on a drug to reinstate us, but what we're more concerned with is getting the drugs that are making women invisible off the market immediately. They have a problem with this. The drugs are making them a great deal of money and they say only a very small number of the women who take them are disappearing."

"A small number? One is not a small number in a matter such as this."

"I agree with you," I said. "They do not."

"So what will you do?"

"I need to figure out what I can do. Dexter-White is a very large company and invisible women are difficult to find."

Ariana reached across the table for the wine bottle. "When I thought I was the only invisible woman in the world, when I did not know how this had happened to me, I thought the problem was very great. Now that I know that you are here, that you have other invisible friends, I see that it is no longer a problem."

"No," I said. "It's a problem."

"You think that we are Chechnya and this Dexter-White is mighty Russia. This is where you must change your thinking. *They* are Chechnya. *We* are Russia. We are tanks and guns. We are force of history. We will crush them beneath our heels like bugs."

"What in the world are you talking about?"

"I have begun to study empowerment and visualization. We are Russians. Do not doubt me. We will bring our tanks to Philadelphia, City of Brotherly Love, and we will flatten them. You don't know where to find invisible women. You find them where you find everything else in the world— on Internet. We will Facebook invisible women. We will Twitter them. We will call them to arms."

"I don't know how to do any of that."

"That is why we gave birth. Children do this. We will call Oprah. Oprah will take invisible women to her bosom. We will call Regis and Kelly and *New York Times*. Vlad says you write for newspapers."

"A gardening column."

"We must stand and make powerful noise that will call our sisters out from every corner of this country. Then united we go to Dexter-White like the force of Mother Russia and bring the pharmacologists to their knees. They will not know how many of us there are. We are invisible. If we are one hundred, we say we are one thousand. If we are one thousand, we say we are ten thousand. Where there are streets, we march, where there are microphones, we speak."

"Dear God," I said. "Have you been working this out in your head all this time?"

"No," she said. "I did not know who I was fighting. I thought I was fighting my husband. Now you have given me Dexter-White and I will promise you I am here to destroy them."

That was just about where we were when Arthur and Nick came in the back door and found a woman they didn't know sitting in the kitchen wearing a great deal of clothing and drinking two glasses of wine.

"Hello?" Arthur said, not sure if he was approaching a burglar or a houseguest.

"Where have the two of you been?" I asked.

Arthur sighed. I was home. Everything was fine.

"I knew you had that big meeting today so Dad and I decided to go out to dinner," Nick said.

Darling Nick, already covering for me. "This is Vlad's mother, Ariana Sawyer. She came to see him but they just missed each other."

Arthur held out his hand and our guest took it. "I'm so glad you're here, Mrs. Sawyer. We've enjoyed getting to know Vlad so much."

"He thought to break up with Evie," Ariana said. "I call him idiot. I said, in what world will such girl ever speak to you again?"

Nick was doing an excellent job not staring but something about Ariana seemed to have caught my husband's attention. "We're very glad they patched up their differences. You know that young people can—" He stopped and looked at her. He tried to start again. "Young people—" He blinked. "Clover? May I speak to you in the living room for just a minute? You'll forgive me, Mrs. Sawyer." His face looked funny and his breathing had become shallow and rapid. "Something at work today."

"Go, go," she said, and then she turned to Nick. "So, you are Evie's brother. Vlad told me you punched him in misunderstanding over mother."

"I felt bad about that," Nick said.

"Never feel bad when you defend mother."

Arthur was out the door and in the living room. "Clover!" he called.

"I'm right here. Are you okay?"

"You're right where?"

"Here." I took his hand. "Sit down for a minute. You don't look so hot."

"Didn't you notice? That woman in the kitchen?"

"Ariana," I said.

"I can't see her! You seem to be able to see her and Nick seems to be able to see her but she has no head, no hands. I shook her hand and there was nothing there."

Another woman might have been upset. After all, he had missed my invisibility for more than a month and then picked up on someone else's in a matter of minutes, but

Arthur was a doctor. He had a talent for spotting problems in other people. As for me, he always trusted that I was fine. "I know," I said.

"So you can't see her either?"

"I can't."

"And this doesn't bother . . . Clover? Clover, where are you?"

"I'm sitting right here," I said. I squeezed his hand. I loved him. In his moment of panic and recognition, in this moment I had imagined so many times, I loved him more than I ever thought possible.

It took a while to iron out all the details. There was a lot that Arthur wanted to know, and while I hit on a few of the major points, I reminded him we had a guest, not to mention the fact that the sheets in Evie's room had to be changed and neither Ariana nor I had had supper. Arthur moved through the evening like a somnambulist, not like his usual exhausted self but like someone in a trance. He poached us some eggs and made toast. He told us to sit there, to have another glass of wine. His voice was very weak. Nick went upstairs and cleaned the bathroom.

"This is excellent husband," Ariana said. "I can see now why you excuse him to me. My husband, when he finally troubles to notice what has happened, he is very defensive. He tells me it is my fault for not alerting him. He feels bad for himself. Your husband is clearly upset because he has been so neglectful for so long." She spoke as if Arthur wasn't in the room.

"Yes," he said, putting the plates down in front of us. "You've hit the nail on the head."

"Tomorrow we launch campaign," she said. "I say we work very fast. Make big push. You write piece for tomorrow's paper. Get this started."

"It's too late," I said. "Too late for tomorrow."

"You call editor now, tell him you're invisible. It will not be too late when he knows that no one can see you. He will take it tonight. Tomorrow we make signs, what you call pee-kit signs. We make T-shirts. We take over Internet. We need slogan. We need to be very catchy."

"Invisible—Indivisible," Nick said. He had just come back in the room and was washing out a pan.

We all looked at him. "So smart," Ariana whispered.

I excused myself and went upstairs to write.

"How is it possible that I didn't know?" Arthur said when we were lying in bed that night after the story had been filed.

"Lots of people didn't know. I should have told you. Seriously, I'm sorry about that. I shouldn't be giving you tests."

"You're invisible," he said. "It's not like you're asking me to name the capitals of all fifty states. It just kills me to think you've been going through all of this on your own."

"Not exactly on my own. I had Gilda and your mother. I had the invisible women."

"We need to hire some lawyers to approach Dexter-White," he said. "Those guys are serious players. I think it's great that you want to print leaflets but it's going to take more than that."

"The problem is I've been thinking of myself as Chechnya," I said.

"What?" Arthur said.

"I thought I was Chechnya."

"You?" Arthur was laughing. "Chechnya? Absolutely not. Not even remotely possible. You're Russia. You've always been Russia."

"I know that now," I said, and took him in my arms.

fifteen

*T*he next morning Vlad and Evie were back. Ariana had texted them.

"But classes start today," I said.

"We are invisible," Ariana said. "This is more important than school. Tell invisible women that meeting will be here immediately. Tell everyone to bring laptop and cell phone. Tell them to bring friends and grown children and pads of paper. They should bring husbands if husbands are good."

I looked around the room. "I'm not sure that many people will fit."

"They stand up. We give them assignments and then they should go."

Arthur called in sick to work. I had never seen this happen. He went to work sick. When he had the flu he discreetly excused himself from the exam room and threw up down the hall. "Are you even allowed to call in sick?" I asked.

"First, I love you," he said. "This is a huge moment in your life and I want to be there for you. Second, I am not about to have that woman see me going off to work."

"Good point."

Irene was in the kitchen making vegan carrot muffins and gallons of green tea. "I sent out a tweet this morning," she said, handing me a cup. "Calling Invisible Women to take over Dexter-White tomorrow at noon."

"You tweet?"

"Evie taught me," she said.

Arthur and Evie came into the kitchen together. Arthur took a muffin and gave his mother a kiss. "I understand why Clover didn't tell me," he said. "But I still can't believe you didn't tell me. My own mother."

Irene shrugged. "When you were a little boy you wanted me to do your science projects for you and I wouldn't do it."

Arthur looked at her. "What in the world does that have to do with what I just said?"

"I didn't do your science projects and so you were forced

to either figure science out for yourself or fail in the process of honorably trying. You grew up to become a brilliant doctor. I didn't tell you Clover was invisible because you had to do the work yourself. I couldn't make your journey for you."

"So do you think I might grow up to be a brilliant husband?"

Irene reached up and patted his cheek. "That's what I'd wish for you."

"If someone had bothered to tell me," Evie said, "we wouldn't have had to drive all the way to school and back."

"You've had a lot on you," I said, giving her a hug. "I didn't think you needed this."

"Mother, you're *invisible*. I'm not *that* narcissistic."

This was news I was glad to hear.

Gilda's husband, Steve, stayed home from work as well and they came over with Miller and Benny to move half of the team across the street to their house so that there were fewer people to step on. I wore a sticky name tag on my sweatshirt. Everybody did. HI! I'M CLOVER.

Benny sidled up to me in the hall. "You are so busted," he said quietly, and then walked away.

Who had connections? Did anyone know Anderson Cooper? The hive buzzed with action. T-shirt orders were placed with a company that knew about emergencies. Nick rented a bus. Arthur brought in the paper and waved it like a flag above his head. Just as Ed had promised—page one above the fold. CALLING INVISIBLE WOMEN, by Clover Hobart. *As of tomorrow at noon, invisible women are stepping*

out of the shadows and into the hallways of Dexter-White, the
Philadelphia-based pharmaceutical giant whose products have
created a nightmare for untold numbers of American women.

The phone rang. The cell phone rang. Nick's phone rang. It sounded like Arthur's office.

"AP wire services picked up the story," Ed said. "It's everywhere. This is huge, Clover. It's nine in the morning and we've sold out on every stand in town. I'm going to want blow-by-blow reporting on this. You're going to cover every minute of it."

Evie tweeted to the American Cheerleading Association. Vlad posted on the Facebook page of the American Hockey League, which had been recruiting him hard. We e-mailed *Oprah* and *Ellen* and *The View*. All three of the producers called back within ten minutes. Lila and Alice and Jo Ellen took the calls. I was out in the backyard, talking to NPR on my cell phone.

"I think at first I was in shock," I said to Nina Totenberg, who was filling in for Steve Inskeep. "And after that, I suppose I had a sense of shame. I didn't know what had happened to me. I didn't know how to talk about it."

"It seems like all that has changed," Nina Totenberg said.

"It has. It was a case of women coming together at the right time and deciding that we were going to stand up for ourselves and stand up for other women. Once we coalesced for action it felt like nothing could stop us. These drugs have got to come off the market. If only one woman was rendered invisible it would be too many."

Nina Totenberg herself reminded listeners that they could get more information about tomorrow's demonstration, and about invisibility, at npr.org or invisibleme.com.

A representative from Dexter-White declined to comment.

The phone rang. It was Wilhelm Holt. "You said forty-eight hours."

"Well, it will be forty-eight hours from the time I left until the time I come back." I walked around to the kitchen window and watched the flurry of activity. Right in the middle of all of it Irene was teaching tree pose to an invisible woman in a pair of jeans and a polar fleece top.

"So the plan is to ruin a company without even sitting down to talk?"

"I did sit down to talk. I was in your office yesterday, sitting. I would have talked to anyone. How long have you known about this, Dr. Holt? How long have you known that Dexter-White was making women invisible and done nothing about it except talk?"

Wilhelm Holt hung up the phone.

Evie had set up our own Facebook page and now Patty Sanchez and Laura Worthington were doing nothing except trying to answer the enormous volume of inquiries from invisible women. They were explaining to them how to work the airlines, the buses, and where to meet.

"Oh my gosh," Laura said. "I have to run. Channel Four is putting me on the news at noon and five."

"Your old station!" Alice said, and everyone applauded.

"Invisible woman on television," Ariana said, and wiped her eyes with a napkin. "I never thought I'd live to see day."

The next day, when it came, was far beyond anything we could have imagined. There were women who complained that it happened too fast, that it wasn't possible for them to make it to the rally, but I think in the end Ariana was right. We had seized the energy of the moment, and by coming together so quickly we sent a message to the world that it would be impossible for invisible women to stand by for another day pretending that nothing was wrong. We poured into the campus of Dexter-White wearing nothing but our INVISIBLE = INDIVISIBLE T-shirts. We locked arms, Jane on my right, Lila on my left, and sang that Phil Collins song from the 80's, "Against All Odds." People were just sobbing, and I mean the visible people, the people who came out to stand with us and show their support: all of the Kemptons and Arthur and Nick and Evie and Vlad and Vlad's dad, Bob, who had shown up at the last minute, and about a thousand others. We had found the place from which we were all lit from within, and oh, but we were shining.

Does this story have a happy ending? I guess that depends on what makes you happy. We brought down Dexter-White like a house of cards. Premacore and Ostafoss came off the market within the week. Singsall stayed on. Suits have been filed but I haven't made myself a part of that. They also say they're making great strides on a drug that would bring us back again but I won't be the first person in line to swallow anything from Dexter-White. I am much more interested in what Erica Schultz has to say. She's leading seminars and has written a best-selling book called *Seeing Me*. It turns out there was a high-profile New York literary agent at the demonstration who had been invisible herself for some time. The minute she started talking to Erica, she saw the potential for a blockbuster. As per the book's instructions, I am drinking wheatgrass juice, which does taste like my front lawn, and taking vitamin D. I would like to go to an ashram someday but I don't know when that's going to be. I've been so busy at the paper I hardly have time for anything else. There is a great deal of work for invisible reporters. Jane has made some real progress following Erica's program. She says on her website that she has entirely visible days. The rest of us have had a few flickers but nothing sustained. Still, we are not unhappy. Lila is the vice principal of the high school, Roberta is working as a nurse. Laura Worthington is actually back on Channel Four as the Invisible Weather Girl and Channel Four's ratings have gone through the roof.

Here at home, Arthur and I have gotten serious about making more time for each other after everything that's happened. We were putting aside some money, thinking maybe we could buy a little boat, but then Nick got into law school at Columbia. We both think that Nick is a better

ABOUT THE AUTHOR

JEANNE RAY worked as a registered nurse for forty years before she wrote her first novel at the age of sixty. She lives in Nashville, Tennessee, with her husband and her dog, Red. She is the *New York Times* bestselling author of the novels *Julie and Romeo, Julie and Romeo Get Lucky, Eat Cake,* and *Step-Ball Change.*